"Okay. Now I'm Ready."

Chancy squinched her eyes.

Well, now, what man could take advantage of such a brave young woman? Cliff eased down beside her and kissed her very gently.

He admired her body with his eyes and hands. And he allowed her to explore him while not at all sure he'd survive such a venture.

She was so curious. "I've always wondered how it worked," she told him with great attention. Having been raised the way she was, she hadn't been influenced by rejection. She'd only been told to wait for the right man. For her, that was Cliff.

He gasped. "Let me."

Well, for a woman her age, she didn't have a clue as to what exactly Cliff wanted. "Let you? What?"

He struggled to say the whole sentence. "Let me make love to you."

Her eyes got a little serious and she said, "Okay." Then she paused. "What do I do?"

Dear Reader,

A sexy fire fighter, a crazy cat and a dynamite heroine—that's what you'll find in *Lucy and the Loner*, Elizabeth Bevarly's wonderful MAN OF THE MONTH. It's the next in her installment of THE FAMILY McCORMICK series, and it's also a MAN OF THE MONTH book you'll never forget—warm, humorous and very sexy!

A story from Lass Small is always a delight, and *Chancy's Cowboy* is Lass at her most marvelous. Don't miss out as Chancy decides to take some lessons in love from a handsome hunk of a cowboy!

Eileen Wilks's latest, *The Wrong Wife*, is chock-full with the sizzling tension and compelling reading that you've come to expect from this rising Desire star. And so many of you know and love Barbara McCauley that she needs no introduction, but this month's *The Nanny and the Reluctant Rancher* is sure to both please her current fans…and win her new readers!

Suzannah Davis is another new author that we're excited about, and *Dr. Holt and the Texan* may just be her best book to date! And the month is completed with a delightful romp from Susan Carroll, *Parker and the Gypsy*.

There's something for everyone. So come and relish the romantic variety you've come to expect from Silhouette Desire!

Lucia Macro

Lucia Macro
And the Editors at Silhouette Desire

Please address questions and book requests to:
Silhouette Reader Service
U.S.: 3010 Walden Ave., P.O. Box 1325, Buffalo, NY 14269
Canadian: P.O. Box 609, Fort Erie, Ont. L2A 5X3

LASS SMALL
CHANCY'S COWBOY

SILHOUETTE *Desire*
Published by Silhouette Books
America's Publisher of Contemporary Romance

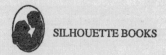 SILHOUETTE BOOKS

ISBN 0-373-76064-7

CHANCY'S COWBOY

Books by Lass Small

LASS SMALL

finds living on this planet at this time a fascinating experience. People are amazing. She thinks that to be a teller of tales of people, places and things is absolutely marvelous.

To all readers

One

People are strange. And among those strange humans, there are TEXANS. While there are other people who live on a variety of lands, TEXANS are probably the most peculiar when it comes to being partial. No matter what happens to their crops or the grasses, no matter how hot or dry or freezing or wet or cold the weather is, TEXANS know they live on the edge of heaven.

That can cause other people to squint their eyes at the TEXAS land and study it. It could well be that it is the LAND that makes the TEXANS just a little bit odd.

Out in West TEXAS, north and a little west of Uvalde, it was one of the ranch crew who explained the circumstances at the Bar-Q-Drop. That was the branding iron's result. A bar with a Q and a drop of something.

Some said the drop was the miracle of the springs they'd found on that land. Others said it was the blood spilled in the land fights. Another said it was the grief of the Native Americans who'd been pushed out of their lands.

The crew head's name was originally Bill, but with one thing or another, he became so stoved up that he could hardly walk and they called him Creep.

Over all those early years, Creep had been pitched off uncomfortably tied horses and bulls too many times. He could hardly walk, but he could talk. Creep had been around for a long time. So, it was Creep who explained anything from the past.

In this instance, it was about the budding woman who actually owned the place.

Creep said that there's nothing like a female who doesn't understand what she can safely do. Nor could she realize there were just things she *couldn't* do. He said that any of God's creatures ought to know its limits…right?

Well, there are occasionally people who haven't any idea as to the dangerous edge past what they can logically do. There was just such a female at the place out in West TEXAS, a nuisance child who had turned into a very irritating young woman.

A clue to her would be her name. It was Chancy Freedman. Yep. That's the truth!

It was her daddy that had named her Chancy. At *birth*, mind you. And he'd been right from the start! How had he KNOWN? Why did he allow her to try anything she wanted to tackle? Anybody watching knew her curiosity was too wide.

It was her daddy, Mel Freedman, that was at the bottom of it all. He just watched her. He'd have to yell at her on occasion. And she'd always try just a little more—until he hollered like a stuck bull.

Mel's wife was Chancy's mother. She'd been named Elinor and had such big eyes. They were like a cow's when it was chewing its cud. Her expression was sweet and tolerantly contented. Elinor was interested in the kid...enough.

Once Chancy's mama calmly watched as Chancy was walking along the top of a picket fence. The kid was not yet even four years old! You know what a *picket* fence *is?* Yeah. And not quite *four,* Chancy was allowed to walk along the top of one?

Her mama said it was good for her sense of balance.

I have to admit Chancy did okay on that fence, and at that age! She never once fell off or ruptured her stomach or gouged her eye on them pickets, but none of us breathed until the stock man Bill just went over and lifted her right off the damned fence.

That was back before Bill was called Creep. He could still move about, back then.

It was Bill who directed the men, the dogs and the horses. The cats did everything their own way. Since Bill was in charge, he was the one that cut off the tops of the picket fence. He hadn't even asked for permission. He was deadly serious and positive as he sawed the top of the picket fence flat. Nobody said nothing.

But when Bill was finished, the boss, Mel, asked real curious, "Why'd you do that?"

Bill said in a rough way, "Because."

That was a TEXAS reply. It replied something but didn't explain, and any half-brained jackass knew exactly why it had been done and he was not to push.

But Mel wasn't that intimidated. He observed the fence while the squint-eyed, ready Bill watched Mel's face. And Mel finally turned to Bill and nodded as he said, "Good job."

When Chancy was little, the only one who actually watched out for her was Bill. Especially after her mother passed away. Elinor had just…quit living.

Four-year-old Chancy questioned putting her mother in that box. She asked Bill, of course, because her daddy was vacant minded. So it was Bill who said her mama was dead. The box was like an envelope and in it she'd be sent to God.

And then they put the box in the ground! Little Chancy was appalled. The whole crew had to do a lot of explaining. She pointed at the mound and questioned in distress.

Chancy would select a crew member, point to the new mound under the trees out there, and she would ask The Question. Whoever was pinned down would stumble around in his reply. They got together with Bill and were taught approximately what they should say. It was brief. And having said what they'd been taught, they waited—enough.

For a while, Chancy buried her dolls. The cats and dogs would not tolerate being buried. It was a terrible time for the crew. They did try to help the four-year-old to understand.

It was the minister who finally came out to the ranch. He told the child Chancy of life and death and made it simple and understandable. And—acceptable.

For Mel there was no such comfort. It was slow, but Chancy's daddy gradually lost all interest in any-

thing around him. That included Chancy. Mel's mind
was on beyond. His grief was deep.

It was Creep that considered it all.

We saw a dog like that once. The lonely dog had
been attached to a cow that went dry and was butch-
ered for the meat. The dog never understood. He
never did. And there was no minister to soothe and
explain to the dog.

The crew made a rug from the hide and the dog
lay on it sadly. He grieved himself to death.

That's about what happened to Chancy's daddy.
After his wife died, Mel just wasn't alert. He seemed
not to be in touch with the world, or to care about
anything. He was alive until Chancy was eighteen.
Guess he thought that, by then, she knew everything
she needed to know, and he just—quit living. He was
a lot like that dog. 'Course he was human, but grief
is with us all.

Creep sighed as his thoughts went on. Makes a man
wonder why somebody like her mother could do that
to a man. Pull him into her thataway so he can't think
of another woman. Just her. Makes a man think on
women and wonder what it'd be like to care that
much. I look at women around here and wonder why
a man would think that way.

But then I'm past the itch.

So it was obvious that raising Chancy had been left
up to the ranch hands. From age four, she'd been
under their directions. They could stop her just because there were more of them directing just one female. They were stronger and they could be very sure

she should *not* do whatever it was she was trying to do that was past her strength.

It's probably because her mother died so young that Chancy never really understood that she wasn't male. There was no woman around to influence her.

She never wore a dress. Her hair was cut so it didn't blow in her face.

She could be very firm. Once she was out with Bill and his horse stepped into a hole. The horse went down and threw Bill bad. You should have seen Chancy take over!

She told Bill's horse, "Stand there, or I'll shoot you!"

Of course the horse understood her tone rather than— Well, he probably understood the threatening tone of her words, and he did stand still.

In the hospital, when Bill was back from being put together and in bed in a room, he looked like he might not make it. But he finally came out of the coma they'd had him in, deliberate. Right away, he asked Chancy with some foggy interest, "What would you've done if he'd bolted and you did shoot him?"

It was an odd question and not clear to anybody else, but Chancy replied instantly, "He'd have limped."

All the crew loved her. Try as she did all her life, at eighteen she still was not even a part of the crew. She was not only incapable, she was female.

Interesting. Her daddy had seen to it that she did as her fair-haired, white-skinned momma had done. She wore sun block, a brimmed hat, long sleeves and thin leather gloves. She'd done that faithfully because way down under her skin, she was basically female.

And she remembered her mother doing it. So Chancy kept that part as being like her mother. But she still felt that she was a part of a whole. In that place, the whole just happened to be male.

As Chancy had grown older, she didn't get much taller after she'd adjusted to that twelve-year-old spurt of growth. All the crew fell in love with her, but she just went on treating them like family. She never saw a one of them as a man. Each was a good friend and helpful. They were almost kin.

And she tried her durndest to be like the crew. Tobacco chewing failed with her. She gagged. For once the observing males had been serious. They didn't laugh. It was only when she wasn't there that they exclaimed and shook their heads and laughed.

Her biggest trial was learning to whistle. Shrill whistling. She could whistle ordinary, but the guys could all do that ear-piercing one when they were herding cattle. They didn't even have to use fingers in their mouths. Try as she did, she could only bring out a little bladder-sounding squeak.

She could whistle a tune good enough, but she couldn't whistle a loud sound worth a darn, and she was cursed with a female holler.

When she was about sixteen, one of the guys was rolled under his horse and ended up in the hospital. Tim had been squashed. Really pitiful. And Chancy visited Tim in the clean, white room at the hospital.

She'd been as concerned for him as for one of the wolf-ripped dogs. She held Tim's hand. He was out cold and didn't know it, but his, uh, maleness rose under the sheet.

The others of the crew watched her, their eyes

amused and compassionate with the problem. That
way, and out cold. Men are vulnerable.

If she noticed the problem, at all, she never seemed
to.

While he was still in the hospital, it was a trying
time for Tim. Beside being squashed, he had broken
ribs. So he was helpless to move as she came into his
hospital room.

That she was there was bad enough for Tim, but
she'd put her hand on his forehead to see if he had a
fever.

He'd raise his one good knee. The crowding rest
of his visitors, from the place, watched and bit at their
laughs. But they were sympathetic. They understood.

Chancy never caught on at all.

And she was puzzled when Tim left them and
moved to another ranch. But sometime later, she went
to Tim's wedding to a charming girl who giggled.

It was not the first time that Chancy had heard giggling but it was something she'd never really understood. She asked Creep, "Why did the bride giggle?"

Chancy was interesting but she was a nuisance.

Chancy was eighteen when her daddy died. He was
just through. Apparently he figured Chancy was old
enough and he was free to find Elinor, his lost love.

Chancy didn't even cry because her daddy had
been so withdrawn for so long that she hadn't really
known him well. She'd forgotten how he'd once been.
It was too long ago.

It was the minister who explained love to her. Why
her daddy had gone to be with her mother. Their love
had been special.

Chancy was thoughtful about love. It was crippling,

obviously. And she decided she'd never get entrapped in such a serious mess.

So it was about two years after Chancy's daddy had been planted next to her almost forgotten momma, and Chancy had no inkling what would come of being in charge of the place.

Chancy could only remember a woman who sat on a cane chair that had a high back and woven armrests. Her mother had watched what Chancy did and smiled.

That was about all she remembered of her mother. She didn't recall anything about walking on the picket fence.

So Chancy was then twenty years old. She'd taken her first two years of college by TV lessons. She was registered by mail and bought the books the same way. She sent in her computer assignments on time.

Chancy worked hard and she did well, but she wouldn't go on campus. The older men had been determined that she should mix with other females who were her age. But she was stubborn. And she owned the ranch. She was their boss if she ever got around to realizing it. They weren't about to mention it to her.

With the times changing and becoming more complicated, it was obvious to the crew that they needed another man. One who could organize and direct them as they ought to be handled. They needed a man who knew computers and how to run the place more efficiently.

Chancy was no leader.

The assembled crew told her seriously that they needed somebody who knew how to direct them along. Silent as her dad had been, he'd at least nodded or shaken his head. He'd been a mute sounding board...when it was serious enough and they'd had his attention.

So three of the men went east in TEXAS to find somebody who knew how to take care of the place. And they were directed to Cliff Robertson.

Clifford Robertson had a degree from A&M, which, in all sports and just competition is TEXAS University's mortal enemy. Cliff not only was born and bred on a place like the Bar-Q-Drop, but he knew how to run a place. He understood men.

In the TEXAS questioning statement, the crew inquired nicely with remarkable subtlety, "A woman who is still budding, owns the place?"

"How old?"

"Twenty."

Cliff smiled. "She'll be okay."

They weren't sure what that meant. But the man was exactly what they wanted, so they didn't warn him about Chancy. They didn't want to discourage him. What little they'd said was enough.

Cliff had green eyes, blond hair and he was a wedge-shaped man. All shoulders, no hips and long legs. He wore boots as a part of him. And he had a good, easy stride.

He knew women. They didn't boggle him. The crew members took him places to eat so they could watch his reaction as the women watched him. He could handle that real easy.

He didn't flirt, nor was he distracted. Women were easy for him when he wanted one. He not only understood and could handle women, he knew how to organize a place and make it profitable. He liked animals. He was efficient and he knew what to do.

And he was young enough not to demand half of the proceeds from the place.

If it hadn't been for Cliff, who was about ten years older than Chancy, she would never have made it to being the breathtaking adult she came to be.

At that time, to the crew, she was a problem. They had to spend too much time being sure she was all right.

Even so, the men looked at Cliff with some sweat in their hair and down their chests and under their arms, and they narrowed their eyes watchfully as he first met Chancy. Men had trouble meeting Chancy. They got a little silly. If Cliff reacted that way, they'd have to find an older man who would be harder for the crew to handle.

Chancy treated Cliff like one of the bunch. No flirting, no wiggling, no licking lips slowly, no rubbing against him.

His eye wrinkles were white as he considered her. The crew expected that. It was a normal, male reaction to her. And since she acted like a normal person, Cliff apparently figured he'd be okay.

However, every single man on the place managed to find a way to warn Cliff. They explained her thinking she was one of them and could do whatever a man could do.

Each man warned Cliff that it was up to him to discourage her pushy conduct.

That caused Cliff to pull his head back and give the first couple of men a startled look.

So each assured Cliff that she would be pushing in to help the men with the herding and cutting and branding and *everything else!* To remember that she considered herself one of them.

And at separate, found times, each one of them told him in a deadly voice, "Don't you let her experiment with you." Their eyes were squinched up and very serious.

They told him that no man who had all his marbles would get within fifty miles of her.

Having seen her, Cliff nodded soberly.

The men went on that if a man was around her, he'd spend all his time rescuing her—from water, blizzards, being lost or risking being trampled by beeves or horses. And they'd add, "Fooled you there, didn't I."

And Cliff understood there was a serious problem.

But then Clifford Robertson moved to the spread. He brought his neat little sports car towed behind his truck. He had his clothing packed neatly. He stopped near the house and got out. He looked around and breathed. His soul smiled. It was as he'd remembered. It was a perfect place.

The sky was wide and the trees were oaks and hackberry, and pushing in were the relentless mesquites. There was a proliferation of wild, spring flowers and the TEXAS bluebonnets that filled his soul.

His room was in the house. That had caused Cliff to hesitate. He would rather be around the men. And he wondered who was the chaperone for the nubile female.

The terrifying woman was as he remembered. A slip of a girl who greeted him nicely and didn't do anything else. Well, she showed him his part of the house and where to put his things.

His unit was downstairs at the front of the house, which was of adobe. The walls were thick and the air inside was cool. There was a separate door to the outside.

His part of the downstairs had been built for her parents. There was a reading room next to the bedroom with a desk, and he had his own bathroom. It was just right.

And he looked at the nubile woman and wondered why she hadn't taken her parents' suite for herself? He asked, "Where are the rest of the bedrooms?"

She replied simply, "Upstairs."

He already knew that the cook and the yardman slept in rooms in the back of the house.

That was all she said. Cliff found a brief surfacing of curiosity in that he wanted to see her room.

Having shown him his section of the house, Chancy took him to the house's separate barn to introduce him to his horse.

The meeting of those two would be interesting for her to watch. Jasper was a big horse. He was independent, curious, self-directed and willing to share. He was an individual animal that was also pretty smart.

As they walked to the barn, she lied. She said, "Here, we trade horses around so that we can know them all."

That caused Cliff to pause and look at the neophyte. So he settled that right away. He told her firmly, "If I take a horse as mine, I'd rather no one else rode him."

Chancy glanced over at him as she considered him with a tilted-back head. "That's a little stingy."

He looked around as men tend to do. He was stern. "It's the way I work. Then I don't have to remember which horse I'm on and what quirks it has. I can understand the animal better."

"You call them...animals?"

He grinned. "I've never ridden a human." As soon as he said that, he sunk his teeth into his lower lip.

Apparently she didn't understand the unintended innuendo.

She was twenty, by then, and all the crew had treated her as if she was isolated and had never read nor heard anything.

The two went into the barn. Cliff asked, "The other horse. Is that yours?"

And she smiled. "Yes."

He asked softly, "Anybody else ride it?"

"No."

He was firm. "Nobody else'll ride mine."

"That's selfish."

He looked at her unduly, with his slitted eyes considering. Then he told her in that soft voice, "I'm selective."

She figured he'd decide on his own horse and then keep it to himself. She just hoped he liked the one they'd chosen for him.

Inside the barn, Cliff looked at her horse with interest and even petted it, but he asked, "Which of these is the one for me?" He'd already decided on the stallion but he could be reasonably tactful.

So she showed Cliff Jasper. He was the one.

The horse and man observed one another, and it was Cliff who went to the horse. Jasper was steady and waiting. And the man gave the horse a sugar cube.

The bribe made Chancy smile.

But Cliff's hands went over Jasper, getting the horse familiar with him. He took up each hoof and looked at each one. And during all that time, Cliff was running his hands over the horse and talking to him.

It was interesting but not unknown for Chancy to watch. The man and the horse were getting acquainted. Cliff was showing the horse that he was his. And the horse appeared to consider that quite easily.

She wondered why the horse accepted a stranger when she hadn't been able to get his attention at all. He'd been reasonably tolerant of her, but he had discarded being her horse.

It was rather irritating to see a man get that close to a horse so quickly.

In the next month, Cliff worked as if God had sent him to them to spare the rest of the crew of the responsibility for...the Chancy one.

Probably the biggest surprise was that she was a jolt to a single man who was diligent in his activities. Those that concerned the place. Without any warning, she was in the group and determined to be a part of it. She owned the place.

She simply did not have the muscle or the strength to handle what a man could do so easily.

She did not obey rules laid down that were brief, logical and few. She went off when she chose. She joined and intruded on smooth work and jostled them all. She startled placid animals and infuriated busy men...who loved her.

It was Cliff who took the reins of the days and the rest could just watch and be critical.

That critical didn't last long. Cliff offered for any of them to take the budding female on—to direct and control her. Nobody volunteered.

Clashes between Chancy and Cliff happened. And some arguments. Those were courteous, so far.

Chancy did ride a horse. Not the calm one Cliff allotted to her. No. She sneaked onto Cliff's horse. There were sharp whistles so that the whole, entire crew all watched what Cliff would do about that.

When he saw what she'd done, he got on *her* horse and whistled at his, who was under her and riding away like the wind.

The whistle was to stop…and his horse did stop. The horse almost had to rear, clear up, to keep her on his back. With his rider stable, the horse had turned and looked at Cliff with some interest.

Of course, Chancy was flicking the ends of the reins against the horse and urging his sides with her naked boot heels to get him to go again. She was earnest and determined—but even her rein strokes were kind. She was simply indicating seriously that she wanted the horse to do as she chose.

That was logical.

Cliff pulled her horse up alongside her and the prancing Jasper. Cliff took the reins from her hands as he got off her horse.

He told her through his teeth, "They are both brown coated. But if you look closely, you'll be able to tell which is Jasper and which is your own horse."

Then he put his arm around the lower part of her torso and lifted her effortlessly from his horse. He had the audacity of lifting her then onto her own horse, as if she'd made a mistake.

She glanced around, but no one else was anywhere around that she could see. So she looked again at Cliff. She tilted her sober-faced head, waiting for an apology from Cliff.

He gave none.

Cliff swung up on his own horse and just trotted it away, leaving her there with her own horse. She was owner of the land. He didn't give a damn.

He *had* told Chancy that his horse was not trained as an exercise horse. He was a working horse. He obeyed enough. He didn't need any stranger getting up on him and demanding other rules. He was not a pet.

The horse, Jasper, was a partner. He was willing to carry a saddle and a man...if there was a *reason*. But he did not take to just roaming without some goal.

Cliff had learned to call the horse's name of Jasper. If Jasper hadn't anything to control or find, he'd get bored and just stop. Or he'd go looking for something interesting.

The horse's curiosity sometimes led to a real wrangle of wills. He'd take the bit in his teeth and just...go!

Actually, Jasper was a whole lot like the male version of the budding female. Like Chancy. But Chancy was more kind.

There were increasing times that Cliff wondered how had her daddy known to name her thataway, right away, when she was born?

From what Cliff had heard, her parents hadn't been ordinary. And maybe not even—normal. They'd been a little weird. Their attachment had been too intense.

But from what Cliff had heard, they'd understood limits.

How come their daughter had turned out as curious as she was? As determined and independent? And yet. And yet, with all that, she kept her courtesy and interest in others.

But she was a handful.

Chancy was never flippant or snotty. She was earnest and curious, and she continued to consider herself equal to any adult male. Any *man* knows no female is equal to a male at any time. Not only females' physical strengths, but their minds don't work the same as a man's.

Men are generally just tolerant and ready to salvage whatever the female louses up. That is done silently by the male with great endurance that is allowed to show—somewhat.

Cliff considered what he'd heard of the parents and knew they had been indulgent. The crew even yet just shook their heads over Chancy how many times?

But it was obvious to Cliff that her parents had never lifted a finger or a voice to Chancy. They'd just observed her with interest…and rescued her if necessary.

In exasperation, the crew told Cliff that the rescue part was just about always. Practically from birth, she had defied the limits.

Interestingly, none of her curiosity was mean or flippant. She just thought she could do *any*thing a male could do. She kept on trying. She was an irritating woman.

Probably the main thing about the changes was that now Cliff was in charge. It was to *him* that questions came. It was his directions they sought. Before his arrival, they had discussed their problems when they were in Chancy's presence. They hadn't really inquired if she agreed, but she had known what was being done.

With Cliff in charge, things had changed. It was odd for Chancy not to know what all was happening.

Two

────────

Around the main house, the trees had been selectively removed. The trees had been cut down and the wood used in the fireplaces when the temperature plummeted clear down to fifty degrees. Once it had gone down further and there had been ice!

There was air-conditioning. It was unTEXAN to use it. When the temperature got up to eighty degrees, it was turned on and left there as the outside temperature went on up over a hundred. They were all spoiled rotten. Especially the cats and dogs.

The high temperatures were seldom miserable because the heat was dry and, if you didn't run around and do a whole lot of things, you didn't even sweat. Men tend to run around after things and to see things and heaven only knows what all distracts them. Well, what all *else*.

At the main house, there was Tolly, who was the

cook. He did the shopping and organizing and made up the menus. He'd been doing that as long as Chancy remembered.

The meals were always superb. He would listen if something else was wanted.

In that first week, Cliff said, "This pie is great. How about an apricot pie?"

And it was on the table the next day. There was exactly enough of the fruit. The crust was crisp. It was perfect. But then all of Tolly's foods were done just right.

The people who cared for the crew ate at the house, together, as a family. All were at the round table on the enclosed side porch including Tolly, the cook, and Jim, who did the yard and kept the fruit trees and the flowers just right. And there was Tom, who did the barn and took care of the horses and of course the chickens.

The chickens were allowed their freedom, and they lay eggs just about anywhere. Egg hunting was a challenge and entertained Tom in just finding the nests.

When Cliff questioned the freedom of the chickens, they all replied in a babble that with the chickens ruling their own lives, the eggs were better.

That was probably so. Cliff had never eaten such well-presented foods.

And Cliff found Chancy was a serious distraction. He thought of her at odd times. She apparently didn't see him as a potent male. That was very different. He wondered if she was flawed.

She never wore a dress. Why not? She'd cut her hair into such a short bunch that she could pass for a teenage boy. Naw. Her chest was female. Even trying her darnedest, she couldn't ever get past that. But she looked like she was trying to be male.

How would she look in a soft gown that went along her body?

She distracted him from his work.

He began to have trouble sleeping at night.

He found reasons to take her along in his plane. That nubile woman was thrilled scary, like being in a roller coaster, when she was in the plane. And he didn't even swoop or show off. They just went up so that she could see the overall picture of the place.

She was fascinated. She found things from a different angle, and she never oohed or aahed over his ability to fly. She accepted that he could and she just went along and was awed—by the sights. Not by him.

Once he told her in order to save himself from concentrating on her presence, "If you didn't hang around at lunch, the guys could talk."

And she replied patiently, "My being around keeps them aware of ladies. It's good for them to watch their language. Then they aren't tongue-tied when they see a woman they want to talk with."

He nodded slowly a number of times as he considered. "How'd you know that?"

"My daddy told me."

"Oh."

But knowing why she was around didn't help Cliff any in his intense awareness of her. If she wasn't there, he could think better. More aligned. With her around, his thinking scattered away and just left his mind on—her.

Actually, it was very strange for Chancy to share the house with Cliff. And she was very conscious of his presence. She accepted the crew, the household and yard and barn people without a tremor. Why should her radar be so aware of Cliff?

She was such an innocent.

Chancy found the occasion and seriously warned Cliff about the cleanup crew. She told him, "Once a month, a team comes from the closest town, Uvalde, to turn the house upside down and clean *everything*. And I do mean *everything*. They never miss a thing."

She went on, "One gets all the dogs and cats out of the house, and one learns quickly to be sure anything one cares about is tidy and put away...first. Otherwise, single socks or perfect, uh, underwear could be washed in—boiling lye? Whatever they use, it's something horrific."

Then Cliff found out that even everything in the kitchen was scrubbed by the cleanup crew. Tolly told Cliff, "I've tried to form limits with that cleanup crew, but that hasn't entirely worked. It's as if the crew was a swarm of grasshoppers. The entire place is blighted when pounced upon by the crew." He moved his face as he frowned. "It's really pretty scary."

Chancy said thoughtfully, "That's probably because the crew never talks. They're sober-faced, efficient...and relentless! But they're the best and most reliable around these parts."

When the day came, the cleaning crew descended upon them, and it was exactly as Cliff had been warned. It was Cliff's first experience and, with the day past and the crew gone, he was carrying around a drastically shrunken web belt. He appeared in shock.

Chancy told him gently, "You'll quickly realize that you have to keep everything in the places you want them to be. Anything left on a chair or forgotten on the floor is in jeopardy."

"Look at my belt." Just his manner of speech proved that it had been precious.

So she did look. It was a belt. Getting emotional over a belt was a challenge. She put it around her own waist and commented, "It was stretched."

Cliff frowned at her and snarled, "It's shrunk."

She grinned. "I'll find you a new one and keep this one. It's almost my size." And she went on off as if she'd solved the whole problem.

Tolly's food was so rich and involved that Cliff's stomach complained. Tolly was startled when Cliff mentioned that he'd like just plain food. That was a challenge to Tolly. And he considered how one could serve—just—plain—food?

So while Tolly made the clever, indulgent bits of beauty for the others' meals, he gave Cliff the basic foods. But, however basic, it was artistically arranged, and there were always celery tops, sliced olives or sprigs of parsley to decorate the plate.

Cliff didn't notice, and he ate the decorations like a horse at a bush.

The next week, Cliff eased back from the table and scolded Tolly, "In another month, I'll weigh a ton."

Tolly dismissed that. "I don't feed you enough to gain even two pounds."

"I can hardly get up on Jasper. And he complains about carrying my weight around."

Tolly pulled in the corners of his mouth and retorted, "You can't possibly weigh any more than you did when you came here."

"My pants have trouble zipping up."

Tolly gasped. "Those house cleaners found your pants and washed them in lye?"

Cliff replied earnestly, "I hope that's what happened. I'd hate to starve myself and then find I wasn't fattening but becoming a skeleton."

And Tolly promised, "I'll find out."

Chancy volunteered, "Come upstairs and weigh on my scale. It's accurate."

Cliff looked at her naked-eyed and asked, "Your...scale?" He would get to go upstairs and see the rest of the house? Enter Valhalla? Actually *see* where she lay—dreaming of him? Sure.

She was saying earnestly, "I really don't think you've gained any weight. You just haven't been careful to keep your things neat and tidy."

"In the laundry basket?"

"Oh. Well, they think they're helping you in washing the clothes. You need to use the lock we gave you on the basket."

"What kind of crew *are* they?"

"Very earnest." She was serious. Then she was also earnest. "You didn't see them."

"No. I was off trying to unstick that da—recalcitrant bull. He was dragging his—belly in the mud. His valuable...belly. All's he did was bellow."

Tom said, "We heard him."

The rest at the table had to agree. One of the crew snorted in his laughter, but the rest were passably serious.

So Cliff went upstairs to Valhalla and was weighed. She said kindly, "It won't be accurate just after a meal this way, but it will give you an idea of what you do weigh."

And his weight was okay. His pants weren't.

Cliff slid his eyes around Valhalla and memorized the layout of rooms. Then he went off down the stairs and out of the house on some ranch problem.

So Chancy took his discarded trousers to be replaced. It wasn't a town, it was just a tent sale at a wide space in the road. They had automobile parts, tractor parts, rope and a gas tank. Just about nobody ever wanted gas. They had their own on their places. Of course, there was the occasional traveler who tried the endless two-lane highway. They were the ones who needed the gas.

In that place, the things they had on hand were jeans and shirts and wide-brimmed hats. They had boots. It was where Chancy shopped. They didn't carry dresses. There weren't that many women around that particular area. If they wanted dresses they went to Uvalde.

The strip shops did have other things. There were saddles and blankets and guns. The guns were not readily available. They were hidden. And they were only shown to known people from right around there. Otherwise, they were not openly a part of the stock.

Once, they'd been held up. And one of the men had been shot—for guns.

There was a big sign out on the road showing what they had and at the bottom was: No Guns.

It was a lie, but nobody that was a stranger ever saw one for sale.

Chancy showed the trousers at the place she could buy jeans. It showed the waist was a size 38.

Pete laughed. "Did *you* wash these." And it wasn't a question. Nobody, who knew her, thought Chancy was domesticated. She could well louse up anybody in any household skill.

She replied in a stilted manner, "The cleaning crew. Cliff apparently forgot to put them away."

Pete grinned. "That crew ought to have a slice of my sales. They get me more business from them than any other way. Most people would just wear their jeans to rags. That crew gets them into new jeans regular."

She ignored his comment and just said patiently, "Give me three pair that are actually 38 at the waist. That'll hold him 'til he can come in for himself."

So Pete inquired, "What d'you want me to do with these? They're still in good shape."

She said quickly, "I'll take them."

"The waist's too big. There's nobody out at your place that can fix these to fit."

"I'll wear a belt."

That was when the word went around that Chancy was interested in Cliff, her new head. That got a lot of good smirking laughs.

Sometimes people just don't have enough to think about.

Her face kind of pink, Chancy took Cliff's shrunken jeans, a new web belt for him and his new pairs of jeans back to her car. She drove back to the ranch. There, she put the three trousers and the new belt in his room before he came into the house that evening.

In the meantime, she measured, cut off the bottoms of the legs on his old jeans and put them on. They were close. A belt did it. He'd never remember that once they had been his jeans.

But he did. He looked at her wearing his shrunken pants and he opened his lips to breathe more quietly. His bottom had been there. His sex had been there. She was in his pants. Boy, was she *ever* in his pants!

Chancy mentioned, "So you recognize your jeans?"

"Yeah."

"I'm surprised. They don't fit you anymore. So I cut these off. See? I can wear them." She lifted her arms and turned around. She had a sassy backside.

She could "wear" *him!*

His hands were back in his pockets. They were there so much lately that the hands both thought they belonged in his pockets. Women are a nuisance.

So Cliff called his sister in San Antonio.

His sister said with an impatient sigh, "Now what." That wasn't a question. His sister then was silent, just waiting for—whatever. Her name was Isabel. She was a year older than Chancy. It was tough being sister to a man like Cliff. It meant a lot of phone calls from anxious females.

So Cliff told Isabel, "You need to come on out here and visit for a while. It'll enhance your attitude and let you see how other folks live."

"I don't care *how* 'other folks' *live!*"

"This will be an expanding experience."

And Isabel groaned, "Some woman's after you and you want me to help you escape."

"I'm not so sure about that."

"You want *me* to help *you* with a wo—"

"This female doesn't realize she's actually a woman. She thinks she's as good as any man and she tries to prove that all the time. She isn't pushy. She just pitches in very earnestly and thinks she's helping.''

Isabel protested, ''Oh, for crying out loud!''

He gasped in admiration. ''You're cleaning up your cussin'. Somebody around I ought to know about?''

''Our parents live here also. They are underfoot. I don't *need* another custodian!''

His voice level, he told Isabel, ''You're kin to me and you owe me for getting you out of that mess with Buford. Come on out here and quit moaning and groaning that way. You carry on thataway and you'd be a bad influence with an innocent girl.''

''Buford was not a mess. You just happened to come at a good time. I could have handled him with one hand tied behind my back.'' And she didn't stop but went right on, ''So she's innocent? If you think I'm going to convince her you're a safe date, you're barking up the wrong tree.''

He sighed with great patience and told his sister, ''She doesn't know to wear dresses.''

''Uhhhhh. What *does* she wear?''

''Right now, it's my old jeans.''

''What'd she—wear—before your jeans?'' she asked with some intent curiosity.

''Hers.''

''She slid out of her jeans and wore yours?'' Isabel gasped in riveted shock. ''What all have you all been doing out there?''

''Not nearly enough.'' Then he just went on, ''You need to teach her how to be a girl.''

''What is she—now?''

''She was raised by a crew and her daddy. He died

a couple of years ago. She doesn't know how to be—feminine."

"In a male crowd like that, who would? But don't worry. She'll come around. Kiss her."

"Well, now, I think that's a very good idea. But I'm not at all sure she would understand if I tried that. There aren't any women out this way."

"Big brother, if there is a TV out there, she's seen a kiss. She knows what it would be. Mother says TV isn't the innocent it once was. Try it."

"Isabel, be a good sister and come out here and help me to help her."

"I don't *want* to come out to some hick ranch and guide an innocent into your bed. I have morals."

"While I'm pristine and pure, I know all about your morals. I went to Fred's that time and saved your hide. Remember *that?*"

"Yeah." There was a silence. Isabel said, "I remember." And the silence came again. She said, "I owe you. I guess. Okay. What do you want me to do?"

With great patience, he reiterated, "Come out and teach her to be a female woman."

"Turn back the bed covers and tell her to strip?"

"Sister, sister, you're a-way off the track. All's I want is for you to teach her to wear dresses, maybe even use a little makeup. Help her to let her hair grow and act like a woman. And get her out of our hair! We can't even talk natural but what she's around and we have to watch our language."

With her eyes then slits of suspicion, Isabel asked in a deadly voice, "Does she chew tobacco?"

"No."

"You're sure?"

"On my honor."

"You haven't brought that honor part up in a while. Tell me what your roll is in this reforming of a neophyte?"

"So you realize she is one."

"I want to know the ramifications. If this is a passing fancy so that she is going to sink me in a flood of tears and the weight of bystander guilt, I want to know *now*."

Being underhanded and sly, he then used her nickname. He said in an honorable voice, "Is. All I ask is that you teach her to be a girl and wear dresses—"

"Good gravy."

"When you meet her, you'll understand. Teach her how to wear a little makeup and comb her hair."

Suspiciously, his sister asked, "Does she have head lice?"

"The only reason I haven't hung up the phone on you is that I have no one else to ask to help her be a lady. Or just act more female and leave us alone to talk like we want. You *can* be a lady when you want to. Momma did a good job on you. You are a lady."

"Why are you asking me to do this?"

"I want her to know what a precious woman she is. Just like all the other women we men are so lucky to see and know. I want you to influence Chancy."

"Why is she named...Chancy?"

"Her parents were—different. Her daddy named her that at birth."

"Why."

"I wasn't there. I have no idea. I like her. I would like you to help her at this age. She is—"

"At...what age."

"She's twenty."

"And she doesn't wear dresses? She must be rather feebleminded."

"No. She was raised in a different atmosphere than you. She has had no instruction in being a woman."

"Where's her mother?"

"As I understand it, her mother died when she was a child. I believe it was at three or four years old."

"Awww. That would be tough."

And that was what lured Isabel into agreeing to help out. She was a pushover for an orphan.

So Cliff asked Chancy, "Would it be okay if my sister came to visit for a while? She's from San Antone and never been on a real ranch. It would be interesting for her."

Chancy's eyes widened. "She'd come here?" She'd never had any female guests.

"If that's okay with you."

And with a totally stark face of panic, Chancy asked her foreman, "How do I do this? Where would she stay? I'm not sure what to do."

And instead of taking over and deciding everything for her, Cliff was quick enough to suggest, "Ask Tolly."

"Yes! That's a good idea! I'll go find him now."

And Cliff's eyes followed her as she went quickly from the room. It came to him that Chancy had *never* had female company! Think of that! For a woman.

Chancy had had no trouble finding a place for him. She'd even bought him pants. It hadn't been any big deal. But now his sister was coming, and Chancy was absolutely thrown off kilter. She was excited. Pleased. She didn't know what to do. Think of that. She'd never had a female guest?

That was a thoughtful several minutes, sinking into Cliff's understanding, then he smiled a little. Isabel would handle it all. And he went off outside, whistling. Chancy would be solved by his sister. Now she'd be busy doing something female and leave the place to the men. They could talk their own way and it would all be easier.

Cliff had read Chancy's conduct very well indeed. She was thrown for a loop. She told the cook, Tolly, "What'll I do?"

And he asked in a superior manner with somewhat lifted eyebrows, "About—what?"

"Cliff's sister is coming to visit. Where'll we put her?"

Tolly was included, that way, in responsibility. So he suggested, "Upstairs in one of the vacant rooms? They are pristine, as usual. That team scrubs them down to the wood and then waxes them. Any of the rooms is ready."

"Yes." It was as if she hadn't realized one of those rooms would be just right. Since she'd never had female guests, those rooms had been empty.

She would have someone else upstairs! And she smiled. She hummed. She cut flowers. That made Jim hostile and competitive. Those were *his* flowers.

He asked the humming woman, "What the hell are you doing? Just answer me that."

And she blinked and said, "I'm having a guest come stay!" And she grinned widely with delight.

"Who's he?" Jim's eyes squinched in suspicion.

And Chancy laughed as she explained with delight, "He's a *woman!*"

Jim narrowed his eyes and asked suspiciously, "One of them I've read about?"

"No. A *real* one! She's coming to stay a while. She's Cliff's sister!"

"Well, what do you know about that!" And he was taken aback. "Are you using the gladiolas?"

"No. I thought the bluebonnets and the firewheels with a little of the fern would be so pretty."

He gasped in true shock, "You'd cut them bluebonnets? They don't last! They're fragile."

"She's special. Her name's Isabel and she's my first woman visitor. I'm so excited."

"Don't cut the bluebonnets 'til just before she comes. They wilt. They're the real McCoy and they don't take to being cut. It's like men and bulls. Cutting takes a lot out of them."

She sighed with great forbearance. "See if you can watch your language when my guest is here?" That was a questioning statement. It appeared to share the knowledge instead of stridently directing. She was not at all subtle.

Jim squinted his eyes and said, "You could take some of the daisies. They'll last longer."

And she had the gall to reply, "Tomorrow."

The gardens were for bouquets. They had always been there. But since Chancy didn't particularly care about bouquets, Jim had become used to his flowers being pretty bouquets—outside. To have the flowers—cut—off—thataway wrenched his heart and joggled his feeling of ownership. Chancy was intruding into his territory.

Jim followed her around gasping and protesting, and she heartlessly put bouquets into his arms and appalled him completely. The garden looked like it had mange. Like a miserable dog that had splotches of hair missing.

Inside the house, there were bouquets *every*where! Even on the backs of the toilet tanks. That was different.

At the supper table, Tolly inquired with great tact, "Perhaps there are too many bouquets?"

"No." She was sure.

And Jim smothered a pitiful groan.

One of the hands said, "I can't see Will."

And she retorted, "You don't *need* to see Will. Look at the bouquet."

"I see flowers all the time, everywhere this time of the year, outside."

And Will had to mention, "I feel like I'm laying on the ground, half dead, and on my way out of the universe. It's like a funeral."

Chancy was snippy. "It's a welcoming to a visitor."

"This woman. What's she like?" And their eyes squinted with suspicion.

Cliff replied, "She's my sister." He'd already called her and warned her about the flowers. He'd told Isabel, "Be kind. She's very pleased you're coming. The flowers are overwhelming. Be tactful."

His sister had sighed and replied, "Somewhere along the years, you're going to repay me this time I'll be with her."

And Cliff said something stupid. He said, "You'll love her."

Any man saying that to any woman sets her back up—just like that! Men are unpredictable and almost always stupid. No tact. None at all!

Three

_____

Chancy was up half the night being sure everything was clean and neat and tidy. With their cleaning crew, her effort was useless. But she needed to know if the flowers were still alive. She about drove the bouquets beyond retrieval. She fiddled and arranged and poked at them so much. Too much.

But she won Cliff's heart. That realization depressed him. He wasn't ready to be won. He was just barely thirty.

He had some years yet to play and look and decide for himself. It wasn't in his cards to be won this soon without a little more sampling and fooling around. He sighed and was bitter.

He moved in his bed and was glad his bed wasn't above hers because, this way, she couldn't hear his restlessness. If she did, she'd smile a sly smile knowing he lusted for her.

He listened but there was no sound at all from upstairs. She was probably out cold. What other 'she' was there? He sighed with remorse to be caught so young.

Of course, he was only just thirty. That was a little long in the tooth to be caught by a woman who was only twenty years old. Barely. Yeah. He wanted her bare. Rubbing against him, hungry with a greedy mouth and excited hands.

She didn't even know how to flirt. She thought all men did was work. It apparently never occurred to her to smile or slide her eyes over or brush against him.

His body got more excited at just the idea.

Whoever would ever believe a man, his age, would be locked in the big house in an apartment of his very own. How was he supposed to bond with the crew? To find out what was going on with them and where all they went when they left the place?

He didn't yet know where the women were around there. He only knew that one woman was where he was, and she was an innocent who was excited almost witless because another woman was coming to visit!

What if she just liked—women? There were people that way. She'd never once turned her head and looked back over her shoulder at him. She'd never even brushed against him. And he gradually realized that she didn't know how to tempt a man. It was hard to believe, but it was true. She actually did not know!

Other than just being around a man, she didn't even know what to do...next. Now that was an interesting thing to realize.

And he wondered if any man in the entire universe had ever had to be the first to make a move on a woman. How did a man indicate that he was open to an approach? Cliff had never had to do that.

She wore his shrunken trousers. How did she *dare* to put her bottom into those red-hot pants? Her hands touched those pants. Her bottom was inside them. Her soft breasts pushed against his old shirt.

By George! She had *one of his shirts!* Now how had that happened? He'd inquire: *Just what're you doing in my shirt?*

And she'd tilt her chin up and look at him over her cheekbones as she sassed: "You didn't put it all the way into the basket and latch it. The crew had washed it, so now you can't wear it, but it fits me."

That's what she'd say. She was stealing his shrunken clothes because he couldn't wear them, but she could. It was like she didn't have anything to wear. But she could wear his old, faded, used clothes.

Ambrose waggled and grew bigger. Ambrose. He'd named his sex when he was fourteen. At best, Ambrose was great bonding, at worse it just waggled and ached. Like now. And the monster was getting selective. It only got hot for her.

What if she wasn't interested in him? What if she could be interested but not serious about him? What if she looked on beyond him...to another man?

Cliff became moody and pensive. There he was, and it was the perfect time for a woman to ask, "What's the matter?" and he had to be lying there all alone. But he and Ambrose were only moody and pensive about one woman...not just *a* woman. That one.

He sighed and flopped over in bed and snarled at Ambrose for being so damned pushy. He heaved up out of bed and pulled on jeans and boots. Then he crowded Ambrose into where he was supposed to be and had trouble buttoning his pants.

He went outside and looked around, bare chested and restless. He stomped over to the barn, and the horses became upset and annoyed.

Tom came inside the barn with a rifle and asked, "What the *hell're* you doing in here?"

And Cliff replied stonily, "I thought I heard something." His tongue surprised him. He hadn't realized it could be that smart, that quick.

Tom advised in a mature way, "Go back to bed. I listen. If anything happens, you'll hear me and my outside gun making all kinds of noise."

See? Even Tom thought of his sex as a gun. He probably called it shotgun or rifle or automatic.

Cliff turned away saying, "Sorry."

And Tom replied kindly, "If I slept in her house, I'd have trouble sleeping, too. It's bad enough being just this close."

Cliff turned back in a trifle overdone surprise and asked, "What?"

But Tom just laughed. "Run around the fence area for twenty minutes and you'll get it out of your system."

"You think...I'm...restless?"

Tom's eyes spilled humor. But it wasn't derision. It was understanding. "She keeps me awake, too. Think what it'll be like with two of them in the house. Oops, one'll be your sister. Sorry. I'll behave."

"See to it."

"Yes, sir, master, I'll be careful."

But Tom stood and watched Cliff. And Cliff didn't want to go out and run around the needed area and go to bed. He went over and petted his sleepy horse.

Tom said, "You know better than to get him all steamed up and eager for a run."

"I was just checking."

Tom assured Cliff, "Everything's under control...but you. Go to bed."

And Cliff said, "I just have trouble minding a snot-nosed kid." He gestured as he explained seriously, "Your advice is excellent, but I'm older than you, and I have trouble minding you."

"You're just like my big brothers. I have to tell them what to do all the time. They never listen. Go to bed. It'll help us both."

And Cliff grinned. "Good night, Tom."

"Good night, boss. I hope you can sleep. We need you alert and ready."

"Ready? For what?"

Tom shrugged, putting out his free, empty arm, "A highwayman? A tornado? A wild boar? A clipped fence? Missing stock?"

"What all do you read?"

"Well, the guys before me who cared for the barn's population here gathered an impressive library. If you ever need something riveting, come by and I'll fix you up...with a book."

"Give me one, now."

Tom smiled gently. "I really think you need the sleep."

"You may be right. But give me a book, anyway."

Tom snapped his fingers and turned, saying, "I know just the one. But don't try it tonight. You'll stagger and blink tomorrow from lack of sleep."

Cliff promised, "I'll read one chapter and quit." He followed Tom into his barn room.

Tom was shuffling through his ragged 'library' and said, "You're a man of iron."

Cliff corrected, "—steel."

Tom laughed. "That's obvious. Here's the book. Remember. One chapter. No more."

Distraction was exactly what Cliff needed. He strode back to the house, slid out of his boots to carry them as he eased inside carefully, making no noise at all. He went into his bedroom and put his boots down carefully and slid out of his jeans. He turned on the lamp and settled down on his bed, opening the book.

He was asleep in ten minutes, his light still on. He slept the sleep he needed and wakened in the morning refreshed. He'd never in his *life* known there could be such a boring book. It had knocked him out.

At breakfast, he said to Tom, "That book is a sleeper."

Now that would sound like a movie that was sneaky great and people would flock to it and pay just about anything to see it. The book was actually what he called it. It bored the reader into a dead sleep.

Around the table, there were variations of: "What book." Not a question; just an opening so that Cliff would continue.

Ignoring the queries, Tom's eyes sparkled and he licked his lips to hide his grin. "Glad you liked it. I've got others just like it."

And Cliff said flatly, "How nice."

Tom laughed and couldn't quit grinning.

So, of course, the others wanted to know what they were talking about.

The two men ignored the questions. They did that as if the book had been lascivious and wicked. That was the naked eyed assumption of the males at the table.

But Tom's eyes sparkled and he did his best to be quiet and sober.

Cliff said, "You're very clever."

Tom responded, "I do try." But he didn't say what he tried...*for*. He just couldn't quite erase that eye laughter and he had to lick his lips too much.

The exchange even had Chancy's attention. She never said much, in a group, but she watched and listened. She found if she talked, the guys shut up and just listened to her. So she was silent or said very little.

Tolly had once told Chancy that the biggest reason the men didn't talk to her was because their language was so rough.

She'd said seriously, "I say rough words."

Tolly inquired with some surprise, "When do you do that?"

"If I lose a calf out of a rope or break a fingernail." She was so earnest.

And Tolly just nodded. But it was clear to him that breaking a fingernail was a seriously ingrained part of a woman. What male ever thought breaking a fingernail was serious enough to mention?

Tolly's mind considered Cliff coming into the house, slamming back the door into the kitchen, holding out a hand and saying, "I broke a fingernail!"

With that clear mental image, Tolly coughed a couple of times to cover his burst of hilarity at the thought of any such thing.

Proving how female she was, Chancy turned away

from Tolly, saying, "If you're catching cold, wear a mask when you're cooking."

Tolly said a choked, "Yes'um."

That was the day that Isabel was to come to visit. When she arrived, fortunately, Chancy was upstairs anxiously poking at the bouquets of flowers.

So Tolly had the chance to hurry out to Isabel's car in order to say, "Be gentle with her. She's spent two days putting flowers in the house. This is the first time she's even *picked* any. You'll be overwhelmed."

Having been warned already by Cliff, Isabel said kindly, "Thank God I'm not allergic to them."

And Tolly sighed. "Thank God for any favors." Then he said earnestly, "She has never had a female friend."

"Oh." That threw Isabel for a loop. How in the world was she supposed to act? And she asked Tolly, "Any quick advise?"

"She's a grown-up, nubile child. Be gentle. She's silent with the men because if she says anything, they remember she's there and their language is very difficult for them to clean up. They're not always aware how vulgar their language choice is."

"If she doesn't talk, then they do?"

Tolly nodded. "She listens and occasionally blushes. A good many of the words they shouldn't use are known to her in some manner."

"Ah."

Tolly explained, "That probably started when she was a tiny girl, and the men working then in the crew thought she was too young to understand."

"Who told her enough so that she now blushes?"

"I've not a clue." Then he said more loudly, "Welcome to the ranch."

His voice had changed. It was welcoming and hardy. So Isabel knew Chancy was coming out of the house. Isabel turned and smiled without doing it deliberately. The "child" was a grown woman and well made. Her hair was too short. She wore no makeup. She was in jeans and a shirt with sneakers on her feet.

And she sundered Isabel. She came to Isabel and hugged her, saying, "You're here!" And her voice caught.

That left Isabel very vulnerable.

Now, how is a woman of the world to deal with an ignorant neophyte begrudgingly when she is that grateful just to see her? When she is that needy of company? When she is that charming?

So their friendship began. It was such a surprise to Isabel that she was wobbled a little. Women were generally so jealous of her that they were chilled. Competitive. Isabel had never been able to understand the root of the jealousy. The why?

It had always taken a lot of careful time before a woman wasn't hostile or, at best, aloof to Isabel. Some never did bend. Isabel had never been so accepted so quickly. She found her eyes a little moist.

So were Chancy's. They laughed together over their emotion—not ever having to mention it.

And the meeting was something precious to Isabel. So precious that it scared her a little. How strange to have dragged her feet and resented her brother's determined request for help...and to find Chancy. It scared Isabel's stomach.

* * *

They went into the house, and it was, indeed, filled with flowers. She smiled at them all. Then she looked at Chancy to share the humor and saw that she was anxious about Isabel's reaction to the bouquets.

Isabel said honestly, "I'm overwhelmed."

That really *was* kindly honest. The place was gutted with flowers.

Chancy put out her hands indicating the mass as she admitted, "I didn't know when to stop." She then looked at Isabel very seriously. "I wanted you to feel welcome."

She took Chancy's hand gently and said soberly, "I do feel welcomed."

If Cliff had been there to witness his sister's conduct, he would have asked to see her driver's license to verify her identity.

The two women talked. They went upstairs, talking. They went into the rooms and nodded and gestured as they talked. For Chancy, the words had been dammed up for so long that they spewed out like water from a hose with a finger on it.

But they *both* talked and nodded and UNDERSTOOD each other! It was an astonishing beginning friendship.

Then downstairs, Tolly went out of the kitchen onto the end of the kitchen porch and ran the iron hand bar around the iron triangle to call the house crew for lunch.

The guys had been separate in their chores and they'd had all that time to think of things to say, so they generally came in talking. This time, they were slicked up, silent and watching. They stood by their places until the two women were seated.

They'd never done that for Chancy. They hadn't ever appeared to be too actively aware that she was there. Since she was around, they took her presence for granted. But they'd always had all that thinking piled up that they could talk about, and they had talked.

This day, they waited for the ladies to seat themselves. Cliff held the back of his sister's chair, and his eyes indicated that Tom was to handle Chancy's.

The men had never really noticed that Cliff had been holding Chancy's chair all that time. Now, watching him seat a stranger, they observed with interest to see how it was done. That day changed their conduct with women somewhat. Well, at least in how they seated a woman.

There was room for other instructions. But they *had* become aware that there might be other things to learn. They just needed to watch.

Tom grinned smugly and did his seating of Chancy with some flourish. She smiled and nodded a thank-you.

Cliff noted that and frowned. He'd had to seat his sister. She was a guest. And she was older by a year than Chancy who was the hostess. He didn't think Chancy had ever realized she was in control of the table.

Well, that she could *take* control of the table conversation. Naw. When she had talked, the rest of them shut up and never said another word.

Then Cliff realized that she had noted that and quit talking so that the people, the guys at the table, would talk, and they sure as hell did. She was very sensitive to be that aware. She'd let them take over and talk. And they assuredly had.

Not that day. Not one of them said a word. They blushed under their reddening spring tans, and they glanced at the women; both were in nice trousers with light blouses. When they'd come into the room and smiled, the waiting men had said nary one little bitty word.

They nodded and shuffled their feet. They'd cleared their throats. That sometimes got attention from a silent woman. She'd ask if he was okay, then he could...nod...that he was. But he'd blush and grin.

Men have it rough, trying to be around a strange woman. All women are strange. God made women a continuing puzzle for men. That way a man never got bored.

Instead, he got perplexed, irritated, needy—in about that order. Naw. The needy part came first.

The meal was excellent. Isabel complimented Tolly on his talent, and he smiled and nodded. The others then said about the same thing, except for Jim, who complained about his flowers being robbed from their beds.

He'd already said the words when the silence fell so quiet that the atmosphere popped. Jim then realized the Cause was right there at the table. He looked at Isabel's serious regard and stumbled into saying with some hostility, "I coulda done a better job of it."

And *she* smiled and suggested, "Next time."

She had him as her slave.

She didn't *want* him as a personal slave. She only meant to soothe his ego enough that he'd shut up and quit acting like a ten-year-old. Men are so basic.

But she didn't reject him. That was interesting to her brother, Cliff. She gave Jim what attention he needed without flirting or blinking her eyes with a sly smile. She treated him as she would a logical adult.

Cliff told her quietly once in the middle of a table argument she'd set off, "Momma would be proud of you."

And his sister didn't even look at her brother as she replied without even moving her lips, "So're you."

Cliff laughed but he rubbed the laugh with his hand. He said, "I thought I'd lost the real Isabel."

She replied sweetly, "I'm multifaceted."

He had to agree.

They all cleared the table. It was Tom's turn, but when Isabel helped, the rest thought they should also. So they did.

It was very interesting, especially for Tolly. Being a cook, he was very aware of personalities and reactions and discussions. People mostly eat and talk and never know what they've eaten. That is agony for any cook.

So Tolly just noted their general attitude and what food helped who, and he listened to what they said. It was in his book to help Jim, who was difficult. Tolly figured Jim was allergic to some foods or his digestive tract didn't like some things.

Tolly was experimenting on what was right for him to eat or not eat. And he inquired about Jim's system.

Jim didn't believe Tolly had any business in knowing about his body. But Tolly was patient and logical. He was slowly getting Jim interested in his own body and the food he fed it.

People are at best strange.

After supper the whole caboodle went out on the front porch which faced west toward the fading sunshine. They watched the brilliant, subtle TEXAS sunset. Of course, it was the whole entire earth's sun, but TEXAS was big enough to claim it.

The crew sat in swings and on chairs and were contented. Some had toothpicks, some sucked squares of taffy they'd helped make earlier in the week and some just talked.

There were those who seldom quit talking. They had so much to share and to inquire about and to chew over. It was a communication fete.

There were those who got involved in the discussions and those who really didn't give one hoot in hell how it went or what was decided.

People are different.

The sun went all the way down and the crickets chirped and fireflies flew and the evening was there. Night. They'd had a long day; they went inside to the living room and watched the news on TV.

There were those who had to get up early, and they gradually went off to the bunkhouse on the other side from the barn.

Tom, of course, would go to the stable. He invited Isabel to go out and count the horses with him. But she was old enough not to be lured. Tom said he had to be sure he'd counted right. She just suggested he put a small stone in his pocket for each horse. Then he could count the stones and know if all the horses were there.

He was exuberant! He grinned widely and said, "That ought to do it! Now I'll know!"

And they all laughed at him.

He didn't mind.

*　*　*

There were those who were jealous that Cliff got to sleep in the house with those two women. Of course, Tolly and his man Fred slept there, too, in the rooms beyond the kitchen. But nobody thought anything of them. They only really thought now that Cliff was there. In the house. With those two women. One was his sister. He needed some help. If there was a disaster, he would need somebody to take out the other woman.

Cliff assured them, "I got Tolly and Fred to help in an emergency. Both women are capable of getting their own things out of the house. It's no problem."

"Yeah." But the sound they murmured wasn't a convinced one.

The men left with reluctance.

How strange that with one woman there, they were shy about staying around, but with two, they felt they had a party and could hang around.

The two women stretched discreetly and yawned. Both were reluctant to leave the room and discard the day. They smiled. It had been such a celebration. It had been such fun. After a while, the hands had become especially sassy and laughing. It was tough to let the day go.

The two women finally said good-night and went up the stairs. Cliff watched them go, and he saw that Tom did also.

Cliff said to Tom, "Aren't you supposed to be keeping an eye on the horses?"

Not looking at a man when he could watch two women, Tom replied, "Ummm-hmmm."

"Well then—"

Tom interrupted, "Hush! You're spoiling my imagination."

And Cliff protested, "That one's my sister!"

"Then I'll look at the other one."

"No!"

Tom chortled, "Hah! Gotcha."

"No, you don't." Cliff held up a hand and was positive. "She's my ward. Being in charge of the whole shebang, I'm responsible for them both. Just like I have a responsibility for you."

"If you're responsible for my well-being, I think you can solve everything right away."

Cliff enunciated, "No."

Tom protested, "You haven't even heard what I was going to suggest!"

Cliff gestured openly, "I don't need to. I know you too well, already. No. Behave. Go to the barn and count the horses."

Tom was disgusted. "You're no fun at all."

"And you won't have none at all. Just go on back to the barn."

Thoughtfully, Tom began, "When I do my thesis, you'll be a vital part." He elaborated, "There will be scholars who will gasp at what I have to reveal about some men."

"I'll read it then."

"Uhhh." Tom hesitated. "Maybe you'd like to read it first and see if the names should be changed to protect the—I was going to say innocent. But I don't know of one clean-minded male in this whole place."

Cliff mentioned, "You included."

"That's why I'm writing this thesis. It will open the understanding of all humans."

"Glad you came along." Cliff indicated the door.

"See you tomorrow. You've overstayed your welcome."

Tom nodded with his lower lip out in a considering way. "I suspected. Tell the ladies I said good-night and I'll dream of them."

Cliff adjusted that message. "I'll tell Tolly you enjoyed the food."

Tom shook his head slowly as he chided, "Well, that wasn't exactly what I had in mind."

And Cliff replied, "I know."

Four

A very few women would be surprised to learn that the two women, who went upstairs to bed, talked. But it was new for Chancy. She was so pleased and amazed. It was so different for her.

They discussed the meal, the people there, who was who and what all. It was like any women who'd been to a party and talked about who all was there.

"Who is...that guy who lives in the barn with the horses? What is his name?" Isabel asked.

"Tom. He's doing his thesis on family ranching. So he's living here free and minds the horses and cleans the stable for his keep."

"He is funny," Isabel mentioned thoughtfully but with a slight smile. "He'd be a handful for some women."

"Tom? He's never seemed that way."

Isabel commented, "Watch how he watches everybody else."

"Tom?"

"Yeah. He's an observer. And his thesis will be a dilly."

"A...dilly." Chancy tasted the word.

With narrowed eyes, Isabel guessed, "It will probably be humorous. Slyly so."

Chancy said thoughtfully, "Now that's an interesting observation. His eyes do sparkle, but he doesn't say very much."

"He's probably writing it down mentally so's he can remember it later and write it down on paper."

Chancy lifted her eyebrows and replied, "If he's writing things down, I'm glad I don't say much."

So Isabel asked, "Why don't you?" She wondered if Chancy really did withdraw so that the men had the opportunity to talk.

"If I talk, it reminds them I'm female and they can't sieve out their naughty words well enough so they just quit talking altogether."

"You're sly to understand that."

Chancy was honest. "I feel sorry for them. Meals are about the only time during the week that they can talk and discuss things with another human."

Isabel was taken with the fact that Chancy really did understand the men.

And as they prepared for bed like two sorority sisters, they discussed which man was named what and commented on their personalities.

Neither of the women had ever had the opportunity to discuss things like that, and they had no background in learning how to do it. How amazing that they knew how to exchange their observations so easily. It was obviously a female gene.

They went right on talking as they took turns showering, sharing the bathroom. As they slid into their silk pajamas for sleeping, each exclaimed over the other's taste in night wear.

How astonishing they both loved the silks. It especially caught Isabel's attention. Cliff had said Chancy only wore shirts and trousers and sneakers.

So he didn't know about the silks? And he'd been there...how long, now? He was slow. Or... And Isabel looked thoughtfully at Chancy; she was such an innocent that he'd been deliberately slow in getting to know her.

How interesting.

So Isabel, who'd never had a cohort so open and easy, was touched to her soul by this innocent... whom Cliff loved.

That was obvious.

Knowing it made Isabel more thoughtful. She slid her eyes over to Chancy, trying to figure her out. Was she aware of Cliff? Could she care about him? He was already zonked.

The fascinating part of that was the fact that he hadn't shared his feelings with Chancy, at all. Obviously, he cared about her, but *she* didn't know that. Or had she dismissed him?

If Chancy found Cliff lacking, it hadn't affected her delight in seeing his sister. Isabel couldn't have wanted a more perfect reception and kindly treatment than Chancy had communicated.

In sharing the same house, as her brother and Chancy were, Isabel wondered how could two people not understand each other? As Chancy mentioned a thing or two about the flowers, Isabel was brushing her teeth. And she was somewhat distracted.

Could Chancy love her brother Cliff? What if she wasn't interested? He'd be sundered. He'd probably have to leave the place and find another. One he'd never like as well as this place.

And Isabel rethought the dinner table and the companionship exposed there. They were a crew that was special. It would be terrible if Chancy couldn't see Cliff for the man he was.

Or—

Was Cliff's sister seeing spooks when there were none? She wasn't sure. She'd have to stay around and find out.

In the hall, the two women said good-night as they touched hands and smiled at each other. Then they separated and went to their own rooms.

Chancy just smiled as she slid out of her robe and lay it on the bottom of her bed. She had never had the experience of sharing time with another woman before she went to bed.

To her, it was a miracle. Someone *else* liked to talk and could do it with her! It was amazing.

In her room, she crawled into bed, still smiling, pulled up the light summer blanket and settled down. A real miracle had happened. Chancy finally knew someone who understood her. One who talked and listened.

And in the room across the hallway, Isabel was similarly smiling and thinking. What a perfect jewel of a woman. How had Cliff been so lucky as to find such a one?

But then Isabel realized that Chancy had not said

anything about Cliff that would indicate he was other than another of the men!

Isabel's mind froze her body and expression as she soberly considered that. Was it possible that Chancy's emotions didn't *see* Cliff? And Isabel's mind scattered as her memory resaw all the men there and their reaction or interaction with Chancy was reviewed.

As far as Isabel could remember, there hadn't *been* any reaction from Chancy to any of the males.

What about her own brother? He was obviously zonked. From dragging his baby sister clear out there to meet Chancy, to the way he looked at her and responded to her, there was no question at all on his part.

What if Chancy wasn't aware enough of Cliff? How could any normal woman *not* be aware of Cliff? It would be unheard of. Cliff was so perfect as a man, *any* woman would have looked at him and *seen* him for what he was!

Then Isabel narrowed her eyes. Could she be prejudiced for her brother? Of course not. Never. But... Could...she? And she considered the premise carefully.

It didn't take long for Isabel to convince herself that only an idiot would not see what a perfect man was her brother Cliff. There was no question. No argument. Facts were facts.

Isabel went to sleep convinced that Cliff would win the flag...the girl...Chancy. Why...had...she been... named...Chancy?

So the next morning, meeting in the upstairs hall, Chancy said "Good morning" to Isabel.

And more typically herself than she'd been, in that

short time, instead of replying in a like manner, Isabel asked, "When were you named Chancy?"

Being used to the question, Chancy replied, "At birth."

"Why?"

Chancy shrugged and said, "Nobody ever told me." Then she considered Isabel seriously and asked, "Don't you like my name?"

"I've just never known anyone who had such a name."

Chancy smiled. "Well, if I write to you and sign the letter with my name, you'll know who sent it."

And Isabel smiled back and agreed, "Yes."

Actually, even with saying "yes" Isabel was thinking no other person she'd ever known would write any kind of letter even *close* to the kind of letter Chancy would write.

So how did Isabel know that?

It was easy. No one she'd ever known could reach up to Chancy's skirt.

She had no skirts. She didn't wear dresses. How about they couldn't touch the top of her shoe? That was probably better.

The two new friends went down the stairs to breakfast. All the men were there...still. They were sitting at the table. They'd finished breakfast and were lingering over coffee. More coffee.

Actually, they had been waiting for the women to come downstairs.

Cliff stood up, and he turned and looked at the others in such a way that Tom got up immediately, and after he stood up, the rest caught on and stood also. They were very pleased with themselves and smiled.

They smiled at the women. They looked so fresh and clean. The women smiled back and sat easily.

The men sat down and had more coffee. They watched the two and listened to them talk. They were charmed.

So it was Cliff who said, "Come on, fellas, it's time to get to work."

And Tom said, "How come they're so late and you're not scolding them?"

Logical.

"I didn't hire them. They can do as they want—you all get to work."

Tom said, "Goody" in a very negative way.

Cliff said, "It can be a part of your thesis."

And Jeff asked, "What's a thesis?"

Tom was very kind and explained that to the listeners as they went out the door and onto the porch. He finished it as they stood in the yard.

Because it was simply explained, the unknowing ones did understand. And for those who hadn't gone on through college, it was a side thought that was interesting. Especially since the subject was self-chosen and should be different.

So the two women were left to themselves with the day. They talked. They looked at the clothes Isabel had brought with her. They discussed them. Chancy tried on some and looked at herself in the mirror.

Isabel said, "It looks better on you than it does on me. You can have it."

That startled Chancy. She looked at her guest and exclaimed, "You don't *want* it?"

"I've worn that dress about three times, and I've

never understood it. I wanted it, but it really didn't want me. For some reason, I don't look right in it. What's wrong with me that it looks like a rag on me and right on you?''

They chewed over that. Isabel put it on, and they discussed it. Then Chancy put it on and they considered it on her.

And Isabel said, "It's yours."

Chancy was surprised. "Why? Are you serious? It's beautiful!"

"It's yours. I can't see why it looks so dumb on me and just right for you. But it's yours."

"Let me pay for it."

"No, no. I couldn't wear it anyway, and it wouldn't look right on Cliff at all, so it's up to you to take it." And she smiled at Chancy. Then she said, "You keep it." And she watched Chancy posing in the mirror and admiring the dress. Then Isabel said, "I have just the shaver for your legs."

That startled Chancy. "My...legs?"

"Um-hmmm."

"I thought men only shaved their faces."

"We shave under our arms and our legs, and any stray hairs on our faces or necks."

"I've never noticed." Chancy was startled. "I'll look." And she went to the mirror by the window and looked. "Why...here's one." She turned and looked at Isabel.

She came to Chancy and said, "Let me see. Yep."

"My legs are hairy."

They both looked. "Not bad. You're so blond, but why not?"

So they used the leg shaver and it felt so odd. The vibration made Chancy laugh.

"You've never done this before?"

Chancy exclaimed, "It never even *occurred* to me! It feels—different."

"My grandmother told me that when she was young, they used to use a razor on their legs and tweezers on their face hairs and it was a real nuisance."

Chancy laughed.

While Isabel grinned back, she said, "Women have it rough."

Back in light cotton trousers and shirts, they carried their lunch and two light aluminum and canvas folding chairs out to the pecan orchard back a ways. They'd hardly settled down when they were joined by Cliff and Tom, who rode two spoiled horses bareback and carried their plates and glasses.

They sat on the ground complaining about being lured out into the TEXAS weather in broad daylight and having to sit on the ground.

Isabel looked around and asked, "Weather? It's perfect."

And her brother said sourly, "It's the overcast sky. It's cloudy again."

Isabel looked at the clear sky beyond the trees' leaves and protested, "The sun's out. It's *always* shining!"

Tom sighed. "Another TEXAN. There was a cloud up there just a while ago."

The entire meal was laughter and bantering. It was fun. And with two men who weren't intimidated, the women talked and sassed and laughed until they had to gasp.

As the men finished eating and lolled around long

enough, they insisted the women be taken back to the house. It was interesting that it was Cliff who lifted Chancy up onto his horse, and it was Tom who lifted Isabel onto his.

Then the men gave each woman a chair and the debris of the lunch, before they hoisted themselves up behind the women on the horses.

It was interesting and thought provoking as the two women were made aware of the muscle both men used so casually.

Tom and Isabel argued all the way back to the house over who was responsible for holding the chair. Tom reminded Isabel with bland humor, "You used it."

Indignantly, Isabel retorted, "But I carried it out there! Why would I have to carry it back?"

So they bantered in the arguing and solved nothing.

And in Chancy's ear, Cliff told her, "I took a shower and changed clothes before we came out. Otherwise you'd be fainting at my smell."

She ducked her head a little and grinned. She liked the smell of him when he'd been working hard. He'd once carried her on his horse when a half-grown bull had knocked over her horse and sent her sprawling.

Her leg had been trapped under the horse so briefly, but it had been bruised and the crew had all been appalled. They'd taken very careful care of her.

Chancy had kept saying she was all right. She could stand on the leg. See?

But the men had said she was in shock and she ought not try it. They were all so sweet and concerned.

Cliff had ridden in back of her on the horse, holding her. He'd leaned her back against him. She'd thought she was in heaven. Tears of emotion had leaked from her eyes over the thrill of his being so close.

He'd thought she was hurting, and he'd groaned in compassion.

She'd been reluctant to be honest but she'd told him she was really and truly all right.

He'd rejected her opinion and told her they'd see the doctor.

She'd gradually gotten disgusted at the idea, and she'd protested there was no *need!*

Cliff wouldn't listen.

The harried vet who made house calls finally made it to the ranch and said, "She's okay. Use a cane for a couple of days if it's tender." And he'd left, yelling, "Take an aspirin if you need to."

Cliff's eyes had been moist when he'd said with a grin, "You're okay. See? It wasn't so bad."

If she hadn't loved him so much, she'd have swung her fist clear around and swatted him one.

But now he was again behind her, holding her chair with one hand and holding her with the other. His horse was trained to respond to Cliff's knees so that he could pull out a loop on his lariat to snag some recalcitrant beef.

In her ear, Cliff asked, "You gonna take a nap?"

"Why?"

And he replied in a husky voice, "So's I'll grind my teeth and be restless and jealous."

She was sure there was something she could reply that might catch his attention, but she said, "We're going into town."

"Which one?"

And she replied, "Uvalde."

"Now, why would you all go in there?"

"I need some trousers."

"You got those of mine that the cleaning crew shrunk." He felt a little indignant. He *liked* thinking of her inside his trousers. And he tilted his head back and breathed just at the very idea of such a thing.

She said, "And I might look at a dress."

In shock he protested, "You wear...dresses?" His voice squeaked up. "Don't you realize the crew will think you've gone nuts? Then when they *see* you in a dress, they'll realize you're *female!*"

"Darn."

That reply made him laugh. He was holding the damned chair, but oddly, right then, it slipped through his fingers and fell to the ground. So he held her with both arms.

She turned her head and said, "My chair!"

He replied, "I'll send somebody back for it."

"I can't have anybody running around doing my errands."

"Why not?"

"Not when I'm capable of doing my own." She slung a leg over the horse's neck and started to slide off.

But she was stopped.

His arms were around her. He was preventing her from sliding down. She turned her head and looked up into his serious face. She said, "Let go."

He minimally shook his head. His eyes were so serious as he watched her intently.

Just think of the muscle a working man has! He was balanced, leaning a shade to the other side, and he was effortlessly holding her where he wanted her.

The horse looked around at those on his back in a

rather tolerant, patient way. And Tom with Isabel, on the other horse, came up alongside. Tom asked, "Some problem?"

They said almost in sync, "She/I wants/want the/my chair."

Tom said, "No problem." Then he said to Isabel, "Lean forward. I can do this okay." And he slung a leg over her, slid off the horse and fetched the chair.

Tom came back to the couple. Chancy was still hanging off one side and Cliff was still holding her. Cliff said, "Don't give it to her. Leave it by that tree trunk."

"Now, *why*—?" Chancy did begin to question.

But Cliff only replied, "There're chairs at the house. We don't need that one...right away."

Chancy's "Oh" wasn't as interesting as Isabel's laugh.

So *both* chairs were put against the tree. Then Tom went back to his horse on which was Isabel, and he levered himself up on the horse's rump and slid up behind Isabel as if that was how everybody got on a horse.

Thoughtfully, Chancy mentioned, "I don't think I've ever seen any rider as slick as you two."

Cliff said, "You've ridden your own horse."

"That is true, but I don't think I've *ever* seen men who could ride a horse in the ways you and Tom have done today. How'd you learn?"

"Uhhhh," Cliff uh-ed as he sorted out women and calves. "Well, you see...uhhh. When a calf is too young or rejected at birth, a man might have to carry it home on his lap."

How many times had she helped in a calving season? But she accepted his explanation. "Oh." And she added, "Of course." But then she tacked on, "How logical."

Cliff's eyes were placid. "The herd men do that all the time."

How many times had she seen such? It had been a nuisance. Carrying another person on a horse was more awkward than carrying a calf, unless the cow wanted her baby back.

By then the other couple was quite a way away. So Cliff mentioned, "You can throw your right leg over the horse's back now."

"Am I heavy?"

"My hands are getting antsy."

"They hurt?"

"Well—"

But she'd put her hands back on the horse's neck and Cliff's thigh and hoisted herself back up enough to swing her leg forward over the horse again.

He was speechless. His thigh was excited. So were other parts. His breathing was erratic.

She said, "Quit blowing thataway, I'm not that heavy."

So he sassed, "You weigh more than any calf I've had to hold."

"I'll walk."

"No. The horse will be offended if you don't ride him, too. And I'd be upset. God knows what all will happen to the attitude of the horse if I should cry."

She laughed. She turned to say something sassy, but her mouth was right there, so he kissed her.

The kiss altered her brain's equilibrium. It also ruined her breathing system. It loused up her vision. And she thought she might be having a heart attack.

How rude of her body to be so distraught. She

looked to be sure Isabel hadn't been witness to such a display with her brother. But she and Tom were gone. Chancy looked up at Cliff with naked eyes. And he was very serious. She tilted her head a little, and he kissed her again.

He said, "You're a dangerous woman."

That made her indignant. "I am? What do you mean, I am. I was trying to get down!"

"You ought to wear a warning sign."

And she was sassy. Did she face forward? No. She turned and looked right at him! She demanded to know: "What about you? How *dare* you kiss a woman that way!"

He smiled just a tad as he tried to lick away his exuberant smile. And he had the gall to ask, "What way's that?"

She scolded, "Just like—"

And by George, he did it again!

By the time he lifted his mouth from hers, they were almost out of the trees. He could see Tom's horse almost to the barn. Cliff smiled. He guided the horse to the front porch of the house, and he lifted her down, saying, "See you at supper." And he rode on very differently to the barn.

It was so very interesting that evening, when the men came in to supper. Chancy's breathing was uncontrollable. She tried to make it normal. What was normal?

Tom grinned at her as he had taken his place next to Isabel. Isabel didn't notice anything but Tom. That's what happened to women. That's what a man could do to a woman.

But the interesting thing was that several of the

ranch men had chosen a subject on which Tom could base his thesis.

He was pleased they'd been interested. It was excellent vocal practice for the hands, and Tom listened closely to each subject. His regretful reply to each was, "That has been done. I'm not sure it was as good a kernel as you've presented, but the essence is too close." Then he said sincerely, "While I can't use it, you put a lot of thought into the premise. Thank you." Tom said something similar each time.

Tom said, "I never thought of that one." Or he said, "Now that shows how curious your mind is." He was very kind.

Isabel noted that part of Tom. He was very careful of other people. It was toughest when they amused him so that he had to bite his lower lip. But his eyes sparkled all along the way.

Chancy didn't hear a thing. Her mental attention, and her body's attention, was only for Cliff. How had she gotten into this mess? Could she ask Isabel for an opinion and for help? Which way?

After supper, as they moved about to sit outside on the porch, Chancy heard Cliff tell Tom, "I did my thesis on ruined land where the oil wells are capped or flooded with salt water. That's when they're trying for more oil. But the empty wells just burp up the salt water and that louses up the surface soil."

"I read your paper. It's one reason I came out here. You did a good job of it."

Cliff asked in surprise, "Why didn't you tell me?"

"You'd get involved with my paper, and I'd have to leave so you wouldn't horn in and try to control the study." Tom's eyes sparkled and danced and his smile was almost uncontrollable.

Cliff sighed. "You're a nuisance."

And Tom replied offhandedly and with no letup, "I'm probably the only one who can help you in this circumstance so that you don't make a complete fool of yourself. Court her carefully. Quit taking all my reading material to bed. Get more exercise. Marry the girl the first chance you get."

"She's *ten* years younger than I." That was a rather plaintive outpouring.

Tom soothed, "She'll never know the difference."

"I appreciate your advice. I'll give you some. Be careful of my sister. She's looking at you with narrowed eyes. If she decides on you, you're in for it."

First Tom laughed, because he already knew Isabel's interest in him. He wasn't any wet-eared kid. And then he was touched that Cliff thought to warn him. So Tom said, "Don't worry. She's just bored." But his eyes glinted and his irises colors seemed to dance with a rather wicked twinkle.

Seeing that, Cliff warned, "You be careful with her. If you're not looking for something serious, you back off."

"Yes, sir." But again, there was all that humor and sass in Tom's eyes.

How was a woman's brother to handle such a friend's lighthearted threat? Cliff stood quietly and just looked at Tom, whose eyes had all those laughing lights. And Cliff noted that even with Tom's attention on him, Tom was keeping track of his sister's movements, there, in that room.

Cliff looked over at Isabel, who was talking with one of the guys. Well, she was talking. The guy was blushing, tongue-tied and couldn't say a word. He didn't know what words to sort out in order to reply to a young lady.

She was teaching him kindly. She didn't just give up and leave him there—which he was probably praying to God that she would do. Isabel gave him choices so that he could nod or shake his head. The guy was frozen, but the experience of participating in such an odd exchange would eventually free his communication.

It was then that Cliff remembered his father saying that no matter the circumstances, all of life was interesting. Look for the lesson or the humor. Cliff was beginning to understand the awesomeness of such things.

How strange that Isabel had thought to help another human being. She'd never before known how to help a tongue-tied man to communicate and, confronting such a one, she'd stand silently or walk away.

Cliff couldn't recall any other time, before then, that she'd considered helping a man to state his opinion. What had come along her way that she'd learned?

And he understood that it was Chancy who had quit talking at the table so that the men could.

Not Tom. He had to bite his lips to keep from taking over the entire scope of any conversation. It must be a real trial for him to research and allow himself to hear instead of personally doing all the talking.

Just thinking of the self-control that Tom used so rigidly, Cliff had to smile. But he looked at Tom differently.

Five

Instead of going east to shop in Uvalde on that day, the two women went up the stairs and agreed this was the day for a nap. They blinked slowly as they smiled, and they separated to drift into their rooms.

All was silent. The quiet wind blew the sheer curtains gently. In their separate rooms, the new women slid out of their clothing and into their soft beds and slept...naked.

Why had each crawled into bed unclothed? To sleep perchance to dream of the men who'd invaded their picnic? Why did their lips smile? Why did they sigh in just that way? Why were their movements so lethargic? It was as if they danced in deep water. Instead it was within their sleep as their movements were made by their dreams.

Downstairs, Tolly hushed anyone who came into the house looking for cookies—or for a glimpse of

Isabel the female who was so different from men. They were used to Chancy and were not as taken with the boylike girl.

One sweat-rimmed man looked at the ceiling as if he could look through it and see Isabel. He asked, "She...sleeping?"

Tolly elaborated minimally, "They had lunch outside today, and the sun made them tired."

How quick was the response. "I been outside all day. I need a nap."

But Tolly chided, "Not today. Have an apple."

Delaying leaving, the hand asked, "What're ya making there?"

"You'll see at supper."

With narrowed eyes, the hand guessed, "You're not sure it's gonna come out okay."

Tolly smiled indulgently. He'd never had an irreparable mistake. He was that good. So Tolly's smile could have been taken as an agreement with the premise of disaster, or the smile could have been a smug knowledge that all would be well and perfect.

The hand chose to think the confection would fold wrong. He said to Tolly, "I'll still eat it."

Tolly laughed softly. "You're a good man."

As the ranch hand took his apple and walked out of the door, he replied to Tolly, "Naw. You're a good cook, no matter how it looks."

That hit Tolly's funny bone, but he managed to nod and his laugh was controlled until the hand was out of earshot. Then Tolly chuckled.

He made no intruding laughter sounds. The women were asleep. But he was so amused.

* * *

As she napped that silent, pleasant afternoon, Chancy dreamed of her parents. They were together as everyone knew they would be, but they smiled on Chancy and watched her as they had when she was a little child.

In her sleeping mind, she watched them back. They made no move to communicate with her. They were simply observing her...fondly. It was with love.

In her bed, Chancy's eyes opened. She was in her room, alone again. Her eyes were wet. She was pensive. She remembered back to the time after her father had slipped away without any warning at all, and she'd been alone.

It had been a shocking time. While her father had been no companion, he had been there. Chancy couldn't believe her daddy would ever leave her. He wasn't even close to being fifty years old then. And he'd left her.

At the time of her daddy's death, the crew had been very careful of her. They'd drawn straws to see who would be around, no talking, but someone was by her or available to ride with her or whatever she wanted. She had been in some sort of shock.

Tolly was the one who saw to it that she was never alone. And he'd found what she needed and wanted to eat. He about went crazy figuring that out and replacing uneaten food with something that had more lure.

One night, she'd gotten up from her bed, and she'd gone quietly down the stairs. She had worn hide made moccasins and she was wearing the night pajamas of silk. In the living room, she saw the night's guardian dressed and sound asleep, sprawled in a chair.

She had gone through the silent kitchen door into

the dark blue, star-strewn, silent night. She'd walked a long way out, until she was sure she was alone.

Then she'd raised her fists at the sky and yelled her indignation to her parents who had abandoned her and left her to grow alone like a forgotten weed without water.

She had had no lightning bolt of anger from them. She had had no message or comfort. There was only the night's silence. She had finally trudged back to the house, weeping, despairing. So lost. So loose from the last of all ties.

It had been a hard, long, isolated time.

And then Creep, the crew head, had died in his sleep. How dared he? He had had the most to do with her raising. And she grieved additionally for his company.

At just eighteen, she had rallied to more earnestly following the men around and trying to equal their work so that she could be like them and a part of something. So that she could be distracted from being alone and in charge. Supposedly.

The experience had made her study the men closely, and that was when she gradually realized the brave facade of the crew was thickened into a shield between them and reality.

It was the basis for their what-the-hell attitude.

They had chosen what they could and couldn't control, and they'd made rules for themselves. They had acknowledged their limits.

While Chancy had understood that, she watched with great interest as, just recently, it had been the crew who had decided they'd hire Cliff. And it was Cliff who was expanding the men in what they could do. But it was Tom who tested and stretched their minds.

How could they keep Tom there so that Cliff could use him?

How typical that in grieving for herself, her mind was drawn into thinking about how to help somebody else.

She lay in the bed with the TEXAS breeze silently moving the curtains and gently moving over her. She felt she was at home. That she had a friend in Isabel who was a miracle. And that she just might love Cliff.

Her life had changed, gently moving into another angle.

Was her life as it should be? Or was she grasping at straws? Maybe she was even steeling herself for the future, in the best way possible. For her, that was to hand all the ranch's operation over to someone else who could take control and solve everything. She gave all the responsibility to Cliff.

Did she want him forever? Or was he just the first man to catch her attention? But if he was not The Man, she would keep his sister.

Not keep Cliff?

She considered that. And she realized that in losing her parents as she had, she was leery of attaching herself to anyone else. They could...leave.

Her self-protecting armor hardened.

When she heard her guest get up from her nap, Chancy dressed and met Isabel in the hall. They talked and laughed softly and ended up sprawled on Isabel's bed as they talked.

The two talked about everything imaginable. They

couldn't gossip; they didn't know the same people, and Chancy didn't know any women. Actually, she didn't know any gossip!

"But men baffle me." Chancy shook her head once. "They are so strange. They decide the limits they can go and they stick to it."

"Not all of them." Isabel sat up straight and lifted one finger high as she pronounced with drama, "There are those who go where no man has gone before!"

Chancy laughed. "Who said that?"

"Wasn't it on TV? Was it—it was 'Star Trek!'"

"I didn't watch that much TV."

"How are you with a computer?"

"Now, that's easy."

"*Easy!*" Isabel gasped in indignation.

"I was caught early, and my daddy got me my own so I'd leave theirs alone. We got a great Apple supply of allegedly obsolete computers and all the crew had to take lessons. This has been long years ago."

Chancy became serious. "But the updates of the computers, and updating the men has continued. Your brother has them all learning the newest means of using the computers. They're lucky he's adamant on it."

"Do you use the computer that much in ranching?"

"All the time. What is needed and costs. It's complicated." Chancy shrugged. "If the men ever want to leave, they have good, up to date skills." And she remembered, "When it all started with computers, I was about seven years old and in with the opening up of the personal computers. I just got to watch and ask questions. It was easy. For one thing, I learned to spell in order to bring up what I wanted. Now they have spell check.''

Musingly, Isabel ventured, ''I think I need you to give me more of the basics.''

''Really?'' When had *any*one ever asked *Chancy* for help? She was exuberant but cautious. Isabel could be fooling her.

But they went down to the office, which was then empty. They played with the computer. They sought and found and lost some of it. They laughed and fiddled with it all.

Chancy told her guest, ''You're not that bad. You just need to pay attention and read it. We're getting one that responds to voice commands. It's on CD-ROM.''

Isabel guessed, ''Pretty soon we can just roll over in bed, by voice we'll direct the computer what all to do, and then *we* can go back to sleep.''

''Okay.'' Chancy considered, then nodded thoughtfully. ''I can handle that.''

They went into the kitchen and talked to Tolly. Fortunately, he could talk and think at the same time, so the two almost-women didn't boggle his organization of supper.

Tolly allowed them to set the table. They were elegant. They went out and found flowers. Jim's voice squeaked upward as he protested another blight on his flowers.

Isabel stared at Jim as if he wasn't balanced, but Chancy soothed, ''We aren't men. We just want a few.'' She said that! ''Should we get some bluebonnets instead?''

That was a tear for Jim. He wanted his flowers to

be admired, on the stalks and in the flower bed. But the waning bluebonnets ought to be left alone and free.

He ventured with some pain, "A little of both?"

So Jim hovered around as the two women sought the bluebonnets and then added enough of Jim's flowers to fill out the bouquet. It was pretty. Even Jim thought that.

And the women had been careful. Not only of what they chose, but of their feet in his gardens. They considered before they clipped.

Jim ended up adding to the bouquet. The bluebonnets were around the outside and bottom. It was beautiful.

The two budding females exclaimed over the beauty of it and the perfect rise of the blooms to the yellow rose that was the top point.

It had taken a year off Jim's life to actually cut off that rose. But even he said it was perfect.

At supper, Jim hardly ate, he was so interested in whether they all had noticed the bouquet. He said, "The flowers—"

And several of the men said, "Yeah. Pretty." And they said that with food in their mouths so the words were slurred. But they *had* seen the bouquet.

They spoke mostly about the bluebonnets. Being loyal TEXANS, they would. But a couple of the men did mention the perfect rose.

And Jim lived through it all, not eating much, but surviving on the comments made about the flowers.

Cliff and Tom both had thoughtful comments about the bouquet. They did that because Chancy had told them to, saying her words from behind closed teeth.

And of course, when Tom got up from the table,

he took the rose from the center of the bouquet and snapped off the stem, then put it through his shirt buttonhole. He almost caused Jim to swoon. Jim had thought Tom was going to give it to one of the women who would put it back or put it in a glass or she might just pitch it!

With the rose anchored in his buttonhole, Tom asked Isabel, ''Want to smell the rose?'' And he smiled. The reason he smiled was because he could control his animal laugh.

Isabel observed the wicked Tom rather aloofly. She replied, ''Perhaps.''

''You got to get revved up to get that close to me?'' Tom's inquiry was lax and he licked his lips. But the men tried to stop the sound of their laughter. Tom said to Isabel, ''If you got to sort it out, I'll just ask somebody else if she'd like to smell me. My rose, that is.''

As the laughter lights began to dance in Isabel's eyes, so did the sparkling light up Tom's eyes. He was a handful, and she didn't mind.

Waiting, watching Isabel, Tom never asked anybody else if she wanted to smell the rose.

But the other guys took flowers from the bouquet and put them in their buttonholes. They looked at their chests and admired the flower they'd chosen. Soon they were all decorated.

Jim said with some blocked, hair-pulling intensity, ''I don't believe you all really understand *any*thing about cut flowers.''

And there were variations of, ''Probably not.'' But then they said things like, ''It's spring and we don't see these flowers that much.'' And there was the reminder that the bluebonnet was *the* TEXAS flower.

Besides that, there was Tom with that rose in his shirt's buttonhole.

Tom told Isabel, "I have other buttonholes if that one's too high for you."

And without any permission at all, her eyes dropped down Tom, and she blushed.

The throat chuckles of the men were a special sound that neither men nor women often heard. There is such a wide variety to laughter. From hilarious to mean to dangerous. And there is the male soft laughter just for women.

Tom stood there watching Isabel and waiting for her to smell the rose. He knew she would...sometime. But he teased her. "There's no other flower that smells as sweet."

Did he mean the rose? Or was he aligning himself with the flower? He was cheerfully, teasingly wicked.

It was obvious that Isabel was not at all offended or embarrassed.

And while the others were calling advice to Isabel, "I wouldn't have nothing to do with him, no how" and "Better run while you still got the chance" and "Are you sure he's had his monthly bath yet?" and "That's just too risky—getting that close to such an animal."

While she didn't take her glance away from him, she did smile at the comments. The men laughed out loud. They were enjoying the whole shebang. When had they ever had such a mix of laughter? When had they really looked at a woman and watched one such be teased so gently?

When had they ever put a flower in their buttonhole?

The men had seen rough worded and slyly wicked

teasing of a woman, but they'd never seen anything like this gentle taunting they were watching then. It was something to learn.

Tim never took his eyes from Isabel as his smile dared her to come closer. He licked at his smile and several times bit on his amused lips, but he didn't say anything else.

And Chancy watched. She was just amazed by such subtle, charming conduct as there was between Isabel and Tom.

Then by her shoulder Chancy heard a soft male voice say, "I got a flower in my buttonhole, if you're jealous and want a smell."

She took in a breath through opened lips and turned her head so that her big eyes looked up at the lash-covered eyes of Cliff. He was watching her.

Actually, he was not only looking at her face, but down her body. And he groaned almost soundlessly for just her.

She sobered and turned toward him as she asked softly with rapt seriousness, "Are you bilious?"

He swallowed a laugh, carefully not choking, and said, "No. You make me hurt."

"Hurt?" She frowned and looked at his chest and face, but no lower. It never occurred to her where he might—hurt—but he was standing and walking so any hurt must be on his upper torso or in his head. His hands and arms? She saw nothing to worry about. "What's wrong?"

"You. You're selfish and ungiving."

She really didn't know what he was talking about. He didn't realize what a neophyte she was. He was paid well. She wasn't responsible for his personal health. She didn't understand what he meant. She asked, "Didn't you get enough to eat?"

And he laughed. Softly. Just for her. He laughed to release his sudden humor. But he began to understand her more. He said, "You are really unique." It was a compliment.

And she frowned. "Different? From other women?"

He smiled and shook his head.

"Because I don't wear dresses?" And she frowned with some feeling of inadequacy.

With her response, he knew she was out in left field and had no clue what he was saying to her. He said, "You are a jewel. You're pretty. Your smile lightens our hearts. You listen. You understand our work. You are unique."

"Different," she said with some concern. All her life she had wanted to be just like the men. Now she was labeled as unique? Strange? Different. It was a little depressing. Her face showed that.

It was only then that Cliff realized how isolated she'd been. She had no clue how to flirt. She didn't know to look at a man with interest and smile. She needed some direction. He glanced over at the stand-off between Tom and Isabel and said, "Look at them. He's teasing her to smell him."

"Is that what he wants? For her to smell the flower?"

"He wants her to touch him in front of all these men. If she does, it'll show that she's his."

"Is *that* what they're doing?"

"Teasing." He agreed. "But the teasing is her way. While Tom wants her to touch him in front of these guys to show that she belongs to him, she is making him wait.''

Chancy watched the two avidly. She saw their attention to one another. His patience. Her teasingly keeping away from him. Their regard and humor. They were prolonging the touch he wanted. She was making him restless and antsy with her delay. How fascinating!

And Chancy became riveted.

Then Cliff said softly, ''Look at the crew.''

They were intense but rigidly controlled. They were riveted in watching. One guy couldn't stand it and left. The others stayed. What did they expect? There was no way that Chancy could see Isabel doing anything rash.

Basically, to Chancy, all that Tom wanted was for Isabel to lean near in order to smell the rose in his shirt buttonhole. She was taking her own sweet time doing it. Actually, why was that such a big deal? Men are baffling.

She leaned over and put her nose to the daisy in Cliff's shirt buttonhole. She looked up at him to show him it was nothing. But his eyes were very serious and around his eyes the sun's squint lines were bare and almost white. His breathing had changed.

Now why was that? He puzzled her.

She drew back to where she'd been and observed Cliff with an honest study. He simply watched her so soberly. She frowned just a bit thinking, what in the world was the matter with him?

Why was he so serious?

She asked, ''Want to smell my bluebonnet?''

''I might embarrass myself.''

That stopped her thinking altogether. She looked

off with a frown as she went over what she'd done, her inquiry and his reply.

None of it made any sense.

He mentioned, "Embarr-ass must come from jack-ass. If a guy does something stupid, he's an ass."

Chancy was again frowning. How had they gotten to this subject? What did it have to do with Tom and whether or not Isabel would be smelling his rose? Chancy felt she must have missed something along the way.

So Chancy looked at the men watching the couple, and then she looked at the couple. Why were they all so riveted?

She asked, "Why is their standoff so interesting to the others?"

And he was honest. "He's male and she's female."

That was the answer? That was supposed to mean something? Chancy felt she probably should have gone away to school and mixed with other kids her age. Cliff and Tom were both older than Isabel, but she seemed to understand what was going on.

That's when it dawned on Chancy that she could ask Isabel! Why, how wonderful! Now she had some-one of whom she could ask questions! It was a great delight for Chancy.

All her life, Chancy had wondered about things, but when she questioned, the men had just said, "I don't know." Finally she'd given up on asking.

But now she could ask Isabel! Chancy could hardly wait for bedtime and find out all the different things she was curious about. Isabel would know.

Finally, finally, Isabel leaned slowly, slowly to Tom and very gently sniffed the rose. He watched her every move, his face vulnerable. His eyes looked naked. He wasn't breathing.

Equally slow, Isabel straightened and she looked at Tom as if she was a cream-fed cat.

Chancy watched the couple in something like puzzled shock. Why had Isabel looked like she'd won? Won...what? And Chancy frowned at her new first friend and didn't understand her at all!

With the wait over, the men moved restlessly and gradually left the kitchen. Some walked on off—wherever—and some sat quietly on the porch, lifting their faces to the west winds, their noses testing the winds for rain. They were always waiting for rain.

Chancy noted that they were quieter than normal. They couldn't possibly have used up all the backed-up conversation they always had. Why were they so quiet?

It was only then that Chancy realized she wasn't the only person who wasn't sure about things and how to go on; others had the same problem. And for the first time, she understood why none of the hands had ever explained much to her. They didn't know, either.

Would Isabel know? If she asked Isabel, would she reply? Or would she be like the men and just say she didn't know?

How could she not? Any woman who could mesmerize a man the way Isabel had just deliberately done, wasn't that dumb. But maybe the men had thought her too young to know the answers?

It was a little wobbling to finally understand that men didn't know everything. Her daddy had misled her and so had old Creep.

Old…Creep? If she recalled, he was only about forty-two when he'd died. That age was getting younger and younger as Chancy grew up.

Chancy went out onto the porch, and Cliff held the door for her. That was different. Then one of the crew got up and gave her his rocker. She had seldom sat in one of the chairs on the porch. But now, she realized, the crew thought she was grown. Finally. They'd always let her sit on the steps. Now one had gotten up and let her have a rocker.

She was mature.

How strange to feel the maturity and still pity the poor guy who had given up the chair. He'd worked all day and was tired. It was he who should be in the rocker.

She got up and said, "I believe I'll walk. I ate too much."

There were smiles.

But the one who'd vacated the rocker to her, got it back before another of the crew could reach it.

She had to grin. And he laughed.

Chancy went down the steps and found that Cliff was following her. She smiled over her shoulder and said, "We need more rockers."

"I'll see to it."

And he would.

That was one of the things she'd peripherally noted about Cliff. He had really done a whole lot to make the men more comfortable. The television sets was one thing. Seeing the world had expanded them. So did TV's expanded reception, the bigger screens.

If Cliff kept on, the men would quit being silent hicks and be verbally enhanced men of the world.

Right then they were arguing what could be done in the Middle East.

She said to Cliff, "You coming here has made a difference to the crew."

"They're good men."

She mentioned, "You are expanding them."

"If you know what all is happening, and how, in this world, you are better off here."

So she asked, "You think Mexico is going to take TEXAS back?"

"Might."

She frowned. "That was a nasty, unsettling reply."

"They were here before we were."

And she said, "Before that, when Columbus sailed the ocean blue, there were nine hundred Indian tribes living in TEXAS!"

His hands in his pant pockets, he looked at the sky, and told her, "For all of time, people have moved around, been conquered, gone on to take over somewhere else. It's still being done on this world."

After a pause, she asked, "Who'll survive?"

"It'll be interesting to know."

Six

As Cliff and Chancy came back to the house, only Tom and Isabel were on the porch. Even Tolly had gone to bed. Or he'd been tactful.

The two walked-out people sat down in other rockers with a sigh of relief. Chancy hadn't known that to "walk out" with someone didn't necessarily mean you had to *walk!*

Their porch talk was lazy. The men ought to have been smart enough to realize it was late and they'd be rising from their beds by dawn. With spring there, the morning sun rose earlier and earlier. Neither of the men seemed to even consider leaving and sleeping. Being there with the girl/women was better.

They just about took turns yawning and finally, finally it was Chancy who was logical. She rose from the rocker and said, "It's so late, you guys ought to be in bed."

The men exchanged glances and bit their lower lips as their eyes sparkled.

Chancy was saying, "...Uvalde tomorrow. We need to sleep so that Isabel can drive well enough to get there and not go to sleep at the wheel."

"I'd never do that."

And Tom agreed, "An iron woman."

Isabel smiled smugly over at him. "So you noticed that." And she was sassy.

Tom turned his head forward and then slid his eyes to the corners very wickedly to watch her with amused chiding. Maybe it wasn't chiding so much as a controlled impulse to gather her up and run to the barn?

The very thought of that licked through Isabel's vitals.

Being logical and used to the men, being around and ignoring her, Chancy yawned and went to the door. Being used to doing everything alone, she left Isabel there and just said, "Good night." Then she went inside.

Cliff followed.

She said to Cliff, "Good night." And she turned away to mount the stairs. As she did, she remembered that she wanted to ask questions of Isabel and learn all the things she didn't know and wasn't sure about. It was too late that night. She'd ask on the way to Uvalde.

Cliff stood at the bottom of the stairs to watch her way up. He wanted to go with her. He was almost as bad off as Tom, but he was older and had better control.

Cliff found he wanted to see Chancy's room. He wanted to just look at it and see where she slept. He couldn't ask to go up with her because she'd probably not allow him up there even just to look around.

He would wait until the women went to Uvalde, and then he'd find an excuse to check the lamp or something. With them gone, he could take his time and see where she slept.

Out on the porch, Tom told Isabel that he couldn't walk all the way to the barn all by himself. It was dark and he was a-scared of the dark.

She scoffed. "Who's been walking you to the barn all this time?"

He was astonished she hadn't realized it. So he told her, "Nobody ever kept me up past dark. I was—now listen, quit that snorting! I was always in bed by dusk. How'll—quit that giggling! How'll I ever manage to get up in the morning?"

"I'll come out and waken you."

He grinned and asked, "How'll you do that?"

And she said, "I'll bring a pan and a spoon and walk around the barn banging the pan?"

He smiled and his eyes were plain wicked. "There are better ways."

"As I understand it, the pan and ladle work best."

"We could see."

"What time?"

"Now?"

She shook her head as she moved her hands out. "You're not asleep! Why should I try to waken a man who is already awake?"

"You'd catch my attention."

She scoffed at him, "Go to bed."

And he immediately asked, "Whose?"

She sighed with great patience. "Yours."

"You want to sleep in the barn?"

"No."

And he moved to stand as he assured her, "Me, neither. Let's just go on upstairs to your room. Be quiet and don't giggle."

She giggled. But she shook her head. "Scat, you tomcat."

"I haven't once yowled—as yet."

While she had to give up a serious kiss, Tom sighed. "I'll go to the barn to sleep alone and scared of the shadows in the dark, with nobody around but the barn cats who crowd me and lick and lick and lick." He sighed with noble forbearance.

Isabel loved it.

He asked, "Want me to go turn back your sheet?"

"I can do that."

"I'd be happy to save you the trouble."

"You *are* trouble."

"I?" He was so shocked.

"Scoot!"

"Kiss me good-night."

"I already did!"

"That was a thank-you-for-the-evening one. I need a good-night kiss."

"Your cataloging is off. It was a good-night kiss. I won't see you tomorrow. We'll be gone the whole, entire day in Uvalde."

"Oh." He settled down to delay her some more. "What all are you doing in Uvalde?"

Standing, holding the handle to open the screen

door but, not being sure that there wasn't one mos-
quito around and therefore not opening it yet, she
said, "Chancy's never been to Uvalde. We'll look
around and try on some dresses. She could use a
few."

Tom tilted his head and considered as he said, "I
don't think we've ever seen Chancy in a dress. That'll
be a shock, for her to start wearing dresses! We'll
suspect she's *female* and not really one of the boys!"
He sounded aghast.

"It's time. Good night."

"I get a good-night kiss."

She opened the door and got inside and hooked the
screen—just like that. Then she said, "You already
had your good-night kiss."

"I did? I don't recall doing that. If I'd had one, I'd
remember it!"

"I remember it. You did. Good night. I'll see you
the day after tomorrow."

He gasped, "It's not even eleven o'clock! Are you
going to sleep the whole...yeah, Uvalde. Maybe I
ought to go with you all and drive."

"This is a strictly female venture. We'll show you
the clothes when we get back."

"You'll change in front of me?"

"No. Silly. We'll let you see the dresses."

"You going to buy some?"

"Probably. It depends."

"I like a cautious shopper."

"I've just bought clothing to come out here."

"Yeah. You look like you're just out of a bandbox.
I should've known. You're probably too expensive
for a poor young man like me."

"Probably."

"We'll see."

"Good night."

"I hope you sleep as restless as I do."

"I'll sleep like a log."

He grunted. "You'd be that type."

Her laugh was very soft.

He told her, "Laughing like that on the other side of a hooked door is unfair."

"I know." And she turned away and walked silently through the unlighted downstairs. He thought he heard her on the stairs, but she was very quiet.

He just wondered where the hell Cliff was and what he might be up to. And he remembered how Cliff had followed Chancy inside. Had he gone up to her room?

How odd that nobody had ever speculated about him doing that all this time he'd been sleeping in the house. Well, so were Tolly and Jim in the house. Downstairs. Like Cliff. Downstairs.

Tom strolled along outside, looking around like men do, and there was Cliff. Standing outside, looking around.

Silently, Tom went over to Cliff. He stood there and was pleased he could surprise Cliff. He smiled. And Cliff said, "What's so funny?"

Tom grinned. Nobody snuck up on Cliff. "I was just wondering why you're outside mooning around this-a way."

"I'm checking the weather."

"Naturally. It's a little late to be doing that, isn't it?"

"It is for wet-eared kids. Git to bed, boy."

"Yes-sir. I'll do that." He started off.

Cliff's voice followed softly. "Keep those cats warm. I saw a mouse out there today."

Not being able to resist, Tom gasped, "A mouse!"

"Try the hammock."

Tom went on off saying over his shoulder, "I can't abide a hammock full of licking cats."

Cliff laughed softly in his throat, so amused.

He looked up at the moon, then he looked over at Tom, going silently into the barn without a door squeak.

Tom actually had a room of his own in the barn. He didn't have to sleep on straw. And he probably wouldn't do that if his own horse could be in his room. He loved his horse which was a ranch horse. The horse's name was Windy. That sounds like a runner who challenges the wind, but the horse just breathed loudly.

The horse's breathing slowed Tom's breathing and put him to sleep. If the horse ever snorted, Tom would waken. There had been no in-barn snorting so far.

But riding the horse, Tom had noted that Windy had snorted at snakes or a strange hand who might show up for some reason or the other. And it was Windy who noted the movements of real coyotes or the kind of coyotes that herded people across the river from Mexico into TEXAS.

Cliff found that he was delaying going into the house and sleeping in her parents' bed. How could a man who lusted for the daughter lie thinking that in a bed that had held her parents?

It had only been two years since her daddy had died, but it had been sixteen years since her mother had left this veil of tears. Think of lying in a bed and remembering the lost love who had shared it once.

Did her daddy remember her mother all those fourteen years before he, too, died?

Had they found one another?

There was all that stuff about people dying and finding their love. Was that imagination?

Cliff became aware of a sound that could have been laughter. They were laughing…at him? He froze stiff, listening. It was the wind? There wasn't that much wind. The night was still and quiet.

He stood listening alertly for some time, but he didn't hear it again or know what it had been.

Cliff went into the house quietly. He even removed his boots, and walked along in his socks. Was he being quiet for Chancy? Or was it that he didn't want the men sleeping in the house to think he'd been prowling like a tomcat?

He hadn't yowled.

He went into his section of the house and looked around. It was so separated and nice that he just wondered how he'd ever been lucky enough to have gotten there and acquired this layout. This place that was his alone.

The "alone" part was all that was wrong. He wanted Chancy in that bed.

Her *parents'* bed? Yeah. She'd adjust. He'd explain that he meant to make it legal.

So he wanted her first?

While that wasn't unusual for a man, it showed a wish that wasn't odd for any man. He wanted her under him, gasping, hot and ready.

He was too restless to sleep. So he put on moccasins and went back outside.

He could remember overhearing a private conversation in a barn when two men were talking; at least they thought it was private.

A younger man was asking an older man how to handle a woman who wanted to marry him. The thing about it was that he needed to know what she would allow...first.

And the older man told him how to do that and what all *to* do so that she wouldn't get caught. Then if he decided he didn't want her, she wouldn't be permanently harmed. And the admonition, "You ought to be damned certain first, before you do any fooling around. It's a serious move for any woman. Pay attention."

Cliff felt that way about Chancy. He wanted her like he had ants in his blood. And he wanted her now. But he was almost positive that he wanted her forever.

However, it was she who owned the ranch. Could he be her headman at the ranch and would that be okay with her? Or did she need a man who was equally endowed financially? There was the rub.

Cliff paced in the moonlight and suffered. Should he? Would she? And he hadn't been in such a fix since he was studying about his approach to a girl in college. And she'd seduced him! She'd *used* him. She was voracious and scared him! He'd ducked out on her.

She'd left notes. The writings had shocked him. She'd phoned him and left notes on his answering machine. She was untamed even in what she said! That went on for a whole week. And then suddenly it had stopped. She'd found another body.

That was all she'd wanted. A workable, male body. Cliff had known men like that, but she was the only female he'd ever encountered who had that voracious hunger. She hadn't minded.

He wondered what had happened to her. If she'd

married? How many times? How many lovers? She'd been cursed with her body's needs. Her need had run her ragged. He wondered if she was okay.

There were men like that.

Cliff wasn't one. He could think of some other things during a day's time. He only thought of sex several times in a day and it was nice, the thinking was. If he was sated, his sex, Ambrose, didn't retrigger for a reasonably modest time.

He was an ordinary man.

What sort of woman was Chancy? Why had they named her...Chancy?

His sex, Ambrose, stirred more. Ambrose got pushy just over the idea of Chancy. How could that be? Cliff had enough to do without having Ambrose indicate to him that he needed sex.

But it was no longer just...sex. Ambrose had an individual, longing lust for Chancy. Was his sex being selective? He never had been before then.

Off, away over the hill, a coyote howled at the moon. Cliff felt empathy for the animal. He knew. He knew.

So he put his own head back and howled at the moon just like the coyote. It was well done and sounded just exactly like another coyote.

Ambrose loved it.

Cliff laughed silently at his aroused sex.

He hadn't howled like that in a couple of years now! Was it the full moon? Or was it...Chancy?

It was Chancy, lying innocently asleep in her bed, unaware a man longed for her. Unaware he couldn't sleep because of his need for her. And tomorrow, she and Isabel would go shopping.

And with them gone, Cliff would go up the stairs

quietly, silently. He'd look at her room, her bed, and he'd open her drawers and look at the silks that she wore under her clothing.

He'd put his hand into the drawer, he'd touch those silks and imagine he was touching her.

Lordy, Lordy, he really had a bad case of her.

So he went off jogging. A man who worked the way Cliff did, didn't need the additional exercise unless he was desperate. Obviously, Ambrose was desperate. Cliff was wearing the moccasins and jogged quietly.

He owned riding boots with the sharp toes and slanted high heels to handle the stirrups. He had normal, flat heeled, round toed, calf high boots for walking in grasses where there could be snakes. And he had tennis shoes. Those he could use on the grounds where the cattle had grazed.

His jogging was a dead giveaway as to his need for the additional exercise. The men chuckled over Cliff's wants, and while they laughed, their laughter was kind. Who didn't yearn?

So the next morning at breakfast, there were only two of them at the table. Chancy and Cliff. Everybody else had gone on off to handle chores. Isabel had gone back up the stairs. In the silence, Chancy asked, "What were you doing, last night, out in the fields howling at the moon?"

His eyes down, looking at the table, he said, "I'm part wolf."

She smiled a little, watching him, and she said, "You hide it well. Do you often go out howling?"

Slowly he looked over at her. Then he supplied a

reply. He said, "I howled because I wasn't in your bed."

Her regard of him became very serious, but her cheeks got pink. Her lips seemed to swell. She licked her lips. Her breathing was different. She sought to control her breathing carefully so as he wouldn't notice it was a problem.

He noticed.

He asked her, "How come you were awake?"

"I was thinking."

"About...what?"

"Oh, just...things." She looked over at him and looked quickly away. "About the visit today to Uvalde?"

His tired eyes smiled just a little. He looked like he'd been drawn, sex first, through a knothole. "You gonna bring me back something?"

"Why, I could. What would you like?" And she smiled just a tad.

"You."

Her lips parted so that she could breathe a little. Her eyes were like saucers. She asked, "Me?"

"Yeah."

So she gave him an alternative, "How about a new shirt?"

"Nuh-uh."

"A belt?"

He shook his head. He said again, "You."

"Well, you know, this *is* my home place, so I'm bound to come back home."

"Come back to me."

Now that was really clear. And Chancy felt that way. Chancy. She said, "I'll be back."

"—to me."

"Aren't you being awfully sudden?"

"I've lasted as long as I could without woman-napping you off into the hills."

"Now, why in the world would you woman-nap me?"

"To get you off alone with me."

She blushed scarlet. She said, "You're being very sudden!"

"I've paid you close attentions. I've saddled your horse and showed you things and you never noticed me."

"Oh, yes. I did." She nodded. "I did notice you." She breathed and tried to seem normal. "I saw you."

"When?"

"Whenever you were around."

"How come you didn't come over to me and smile at me?"

"I wasn't sure you noticed me."

"I noticed."

She smiled and blushed and she tried to breathe normally. She said, "If you're just teasing, you're being unkind."

He lifted his face a little as his sunken eyes came to her and he just looked at her. He looked like an abandoned dog. One who had no home, and he was lost.

It was perfect.

He didn't realize how used he looked. How worn. He had no idea how she wanted to heal him. It was well done and he didn't even know it was so!

She said, "I've promised your sister that I'd go shopping with her. I'm going to buy a dress."

He nodded soberly.

"I will come back."

"I'll wait."

"This is very unsettling. Are you teasing me?"

"No."

"I'm not certain. No one has ever acted this way with me before and I'm not at all sure how to behave."

His eyes smiled a little. "Do you know about misbehaving?"

She shook her head. "I've always tried just to be a part of the crew. I don't know how to be any other way."

And his heart was touched. He'd been treating her like any woman. He'd forgotten how raw and unused she was. His smile was gentle. He told her, "Don't worry. It'll all be okay. I promise."

Men are born with those sayings tattooed inside their skulls.

Cliff had hurried to soothe Chancy because he'd heard his sister's footsteps upstairs in the hall.

Isabel came down the stairs wearing heelless shoes, a blouse and trousers because that was all that Chancy had to wear. Isabel didn't want Chancy thinking she was different and not like every other woman.

After greeting his sister, Cliff walked the two women out to the car. His hands were in his pant pockets.

Isabel asked Chancy, "Do you want to drive?"

Chancy gasped in delight. She grinned and said, "Yes!" Then she asked, "You really mean I can?"

"Of course. You know the area."

"The men always drive me. It's such a bore. But they never let me drive if they're in the car."

"I have a brother like that." Isabel slid her eyes over to Cliff.

Cliff was earnest. "Just be glad you get to drive, Chancy. That Isabel is hell on wheels! The warning sirens wail when she leaves the driveway at home. Everybody around knows it's either tornadoes or Isabel driving. But it makes them alert."

Chancy tried not to smile. She asked sassily of Isabel, "Is that true?"

And while Cliff said an emphatic, "Yes!" Isabel lifted her eyebrows and said a distinct, "No."

So Isabel got into the passenger seat, and Chancy got behind the wheel. Cliff closed her car door and asked, "You got a driver's license?"

Snubbingly, Chancy said, "Yep."

"You buy it through some cheesy magazine?"

"I took the tests."

Cliff squinted, "And you *passed?*"

"No problem."

So he urged, "Don't start the car until I get to the porch."

She turned the ignition key and revved up the motor, which made him clamp one hand on top of his hat as he ran for the porch.

Both women laughed. They looked at each other with adult tolerance and grinned. Even Chancy slowly shook her head, but still she grinned.

She honked twice as she again revved up the motor and turned in an excellent circle before she bounced the car gently over the rough road until they got to the main stem going out to the cement road.

Cliff stood at the top of the porch steps and watched from under his brim as the car's size slowly dwindled as she left him. She wasn't going somewhere, she was leaving him there alone.

He could see the dot of the car as it came to the highway. She hesitated, obviously looking both ways, and then she turned with skill onto the road and drove away from him.

That was how it felt to have her go somewhere without him. She went away from him. He suspected he had a very bad case of her. It had started when he first saw her about six months ago.

If it hadn't been for Chancy, he'd have never accepted the job as foreman. The place was too far away from everything. It surprised him that they had a crew there. How'd they keep such men in such an isolated place? He'd found that they were all good friends, and the headmen had been easy on the crew.

Just like everywhere else in the world, it all depended on courtesy. They were all paid well. That was probably thought about first, but after being there, it was the treatment and courtesy that kept the men there.

And Cliff thought yet again that what the men needed was women. No, not that kind, real women for wives. They ought to invite some over for a picnic and just let them visit.

It was obvious that Chancy didn't have any women friends. So Cliff wondered if any of the men knew of families around? He'd find out.

She was gone. He looked down the road. Chancy was out of sight. So was his sister, but he didn't think about her being gone. It was only that Chancy was no longer there.

—and now he could go up and see her room.

Tom called, "We got a sick horse."

Cliff stood there on the porch. If he went to check out a horse that Tom said was sick, he'd probably never get to see that room where Chancy slept. Changed clothes. Stripped naked. Admired herself in the mirror.

Did a mirror save images?

He called to Tom, "I'll call the vet. Isolate the horse. Clean his stall. Keep the other horses away from it."

Tom stood still for a minute and then said, "Right."

So Cliff did call the vet. His assistant, who was his wife, said, "He's just out west of you. Call him at Earl Nance's right away and he'll come on by your place on his way home." And she hung up.

Why couldn't she call her husband? So Cliff called the number and the Nance who answered questioned the caller, well, hello and what all had he been doing and what all had they heard around and about and how were the fields?

Cliff said instead, "I need to talk to the vet. We got a sick horse."

"Oh? What all's wrong with it?"

"Earl, just get the vet before he takes off and I can't find him again."

"Okay. We'll visit another time. You all home to-morrow?"

"More than likely."

"Clara's heard you got company. We'll come on over about noon. Right in time for lunch."

"How surprising." Then Cliff actually ran all the words together. "Get-me-the-vet."

"Right now. Everything else okay?"

Through his teeth, Cliff said, "Fine. Come on, Earl, call the vet to the phone."

"Oh, sure. Hey, Charlie? Is the vet still here? Well, blow the tornado warning and get him back!"

That took a while. Everybody else along the line got on the phone and talked and questioned and visited. The vet did finally get on the line and several of those on the phone began to ask him questions about their flocks or horses or whatever, but Cliff was adamant. He bellowed, "This is *my* call! We've got a sick horse."

And the vet said calmly, "You're on my way in, I'll come on by."

Cliff said, "We'll be looking for you. Don't stop anywhere for lunch, we'll have it here."

"Thank you."

And the vet hung up. Not everyone else did. They began to visit. But Cliff hung up the phone gently.

People are strange. They are so amazing and so wonderful and so weird!

Cliff turned away from the phone and headed for the back door.

Then he stopped. He looked around at the empty, silent place. No one was anywhere around.

He turned quietly and went through the living room into the hall and there was the staircase. No one was on it. He could go up the stairs and into her room.

He listened. There was no sound. He quietly mounted the stairs and he held his breath. No one came in looking for him.

He reached the upper hall and paused looking only at her door. He went silently into her room. It was neat and orderly. It was hers.

Her silk pajamas were across her made bed. Cliff picked them up. He could pull them through a ring, they were so fragile. He lifted them to his face and he could breathe the essence of her skin.

By the time he got down to the barn, the vet was already there. He said, "She got some loco weed. I've made her throw up. She'll be okay. She isn't gonna give the other animals anything."

He called to Jim of the house crew, "Hey, Jim? Could you burn that stuff? You don't want that seed taking root around here. Where'd she get that?"

And Cliff said, "That's what we get for letting a greenhorn like Tom go off by hisself. He couldn't even recognize loco weed."

Seven

The day was another perfect TEXAS day. The two women talked and laughed as Chancy drove Isabel's car down the two-lane highway. They met very little traffic.

Isabel couldn't stop her tongue. She asked, "What do you think of my brother?"

Chancy replied immediately. "We've always wanted such an organized man. We're so far out that it's hard to get a good crew. We solved that by paying them more. But Cliff is superior.

"He has been serious in getting the men on more advanced computers. They're learning the resources. TEXAS University is especially accessible to ranchers. So is A&M but I'm partial to TEXAS U."

She hastened to add, "I do realize it is now called the University of TEXAS, but my granddaddy went there when it was still called TEXAS first without any words ahead of it, as is only right.''

She turned her head briefly to exchange a smug TEXAS look with Isabel, who said, ''Amen.''

Isabel told Chancy, ''You're a fooler.''

Chancy smiled. ''Not at all. I've told you how the men became conscious of the words they use and it tied their tongues. They're alone too much. They have all this conversation piled up inside them and they really need to talk.''

Isabel nodded. ''Yeah.'' She looked at Chancy as they rode along. And she said with deeper understanding, ''You're a nice woman.''

Chancy grinned and cast a quick glance at her passenger. ''And you're a miracle. How I've longed for a woman friend.''

Isabel laughed in her throat. ''I have to tell you this. But before you make me a saint, you need to know that I dreaded coming out and meeting you.''

''Why? You needed to visit with your brother.''

''He asked me to come out and see you.''

''To—see—me?''

And Isabel thought: uh-oh. But she said smoothly, ''He believes you're special and he wanted me to see you also.''

Chancy laughed. ''Out this far in the wilds of west TEXAS, you thought he was desperate and although I *was* female, I was cockeyed, wild and woolly, and he'd been out here too long?''

That let Isabel slide out of confidences, ''That about covers it. I found a friend.''

Chancy said, ''But you were in the city and had friends. I didn't have any woman around here! You're a miracle!'' She grinned at Isabel briefly before again watching the road.

So Isabel explained, "Actually," she didn't lie. She was honest. "I'm a witch of a woman. I'm selfish and hard to get along with, and Cliff wanted me to take after you and learn how kind you are."

When Chancy finished laughing, the laughter being so that she'd had to slow down the car, she asked, "And now you understand that I'm perfect. Right?"

"Damned near. You scare me a little. You terrify Cliff."

That set Chancy off into more laughter. She discarded that Isabel might be serious.

It took a while to go south and east to Uvalde. The roads were just about empty. The trees were almost entirely mesquite and not very tall. The fences were barbed wire, which TEXANS call "bob" wire. And if one wasn't driving the car and could look carefully, there were deer standing back a-ways who watched them pass.

There were cattle here and there in the lacy trees. Even two-laned, the road was the usual perfect TEXAS road.

However, they came to a crossroad that was organized with traffic lights. And there was no other car, Chancy looked, but she didn't actually register the red light. She went on through.

Isabel asked in shock, "Didn't you see the red light?"

"Is this a—red light district?"

"No. The *traffic* light!"

"Where?"

"Back at the crossroad."

"A traffic light?"

"Don't you know about traffic lights?"

"What are they?"

"My word!" Isabel gasped. "Pull over. We need to change seats."

"Why?"

"Cops get upset if people go through traffic lights. Other cars slam on their brakes, but they aren't always quick enough."

"Red is for danger?"

"Yes."

"Oh," she said. "I recall something like that." Then she added, "That's logical." She pulled to the side of the road. "We don't have those things out where I live."

"Haven't you ever seen them on TV?"

Chancy considered. "I don't remember that anyone called attention to them."

"How'd you get your license? You...do have a license?"

Chancy replied, "Of course. I drove Mr. Soper around, and he said I'd done a right good job of it." She got out of the car and went around to the other side.

Isabel slid over the middle hump, onto the driver's seat and under the wheel.

As the aptly named Chancy slid in on the passenger side, Isabel said, "It never occurred to me that you wouldn't know about traffic lights. Watch as we go along. Red is for stop and green is for go. Yellow means the light is changing. It's best to stop with a yellow light. Watch. Then you can drive back, if you like."

"Who ever heard of traffic lights?"

"So you've never been to Uvalde before?"

"No."

Isabel was fascinated. "Where do you find clothing?"

"I buy my clothes on a road where there are tents instead of stores. You'd love it. They are reasonably priced."

"How fascinating." And Isabel drove carefully into Uvalde. There were traffic lights. Isabel called Chancy's attention to them.

The town was fascinating. Lovely.

It is a charming town. It is preserved and cared for. The trees are big and old and trimmed.

The downtown buildings are charming. There is a wicked Pan on a roof point of one of the preserved buildings. The residential area is cared for and used carefully. Like the houses, the yards are neat and tidy.

The people are welcoming and friendly in the TEXAS manner. They don't seem to realize people are strangers. They're just more people to know.

Isabel parked the car, and they got out and stood looking around. They grinned at each other, then they went to a bookstore and chose some to buy and store in the waiting car.

Getting that vital purchase out of the way, they began to look at clothing. They tried several stores in comparison. And they went back to the second one where they discussed and considered the clothes. The dresses, slips, bras...that sort of things.

Interestingly, Isabel was very aware that tastes differ, and what looks good on one person can be a disaster on another. She was careful.

But so was Chancy. That was the surprise. However, there are magazines which show clothing, and

Chancy had been aware enough, and longing enough to want certain things.

Some clothes were obviously wrong for her. Isabel didn't immediately discard any unsuitable garments Chancy put on. It was Chancy who considered and compared.

It all took time.

There were five outfits put aside. Chancy wanted them all. Isabel was not sure of two of them.

They went to a delightful sandwich bar, which was in a drugstore, and they had lunch. It was perfect. Everybody talked to everybody else.

Chancy met a woman she'd talked to any number of times on the phone and on the communication radio. The contacts had been a circuit of information about cattle rustling or fires or something else loose or dangerous.

The two women were astonished to meet face to face and the only reason they did was that Isabel had called Chancy's name. Now, how many people have that name?

So the two visitors were introduced around. There was laughter and exclamations. "I remember that!" and "But you found it!" and "That was scary. You handled it well."

It was like old home week. And Isabel listened and smiled softly. It was interesting to see Chancy bloom in the exchange. She handled herself so well that Isabel wondered how she'd managed to be so silent at the ranch.

Of course, Chancy had told her that only her silence allowed the men to forget her and talk. Think of the backed up ideas and opinions she'd smothered.

Isabel looked at Chancy with growing admiration.

And she remembered how she hadn't wanted to go to the ranch and deal with a half-brained dummy.

That was the ''dummy'' over there, talking, laughing, bragging on someone else's conduct. She was a whole woman.

Isabel wondered: would Cliff be able to keep up with Chancy? He thought she was so quiet and withdrawn that he'd have to be the one to help her along.

How droll.

How many women would have done what Chancy had when she silenced herself so that others had the courage to talk. Then to keep from interfering or silencing them, Chancy had listened and not put her oar into the stream of conversation.

A listener.

A woman who could withdraw so that the men need not watch their language or stumble over the words and search for an acceptable replacement for the ones they used so easily among men.

Then Isabel thought of Cliff, who was guiding the men into communication via the computers. On line, they had to watch their language. In that way, they would gradually be careful of how they said what.

So while Chancy had hushed herself so that the men could talk, it was Cliff giving them reason to watch what they said. It was Cliff who was teaching them to communicate with acceptable language. How interesting is the computer. How leveling it is for us all. Rising for some, lowering for others. All of it helping in reaching for an acceptable standard.

So after their very extended lunch, the two women strolled along the walks under big old oak trees in downtown Uvalde. Even then, there were people who called to Chancy. "I hear you're the one I talk to on the CB?" The TEXAS questioning statement.

Chancy laughed. "The bull?"

"Naw. It was that damned calf looking for his mama."

Chancy chided, "You should have kept her."

"You gotta meet my woman. She's gettin' a soda at the drug store. Come along." He gestured.

"I've already talked to her. We were at the drug store for lunch."

The husband grinned. "I bet she was surprised by you. You sound like a solid woman on the air. You're just a little girl."

Chancy tilted back her head and declared, "I'm a woman!"

But the man just laughed as he waved a goodbye.

Isabel commented, "You must know the whole, entire town."

"It isn't just this town, but the whole area. We're a community because of the CB's."

Isabel mentioned, "The men ought to come into town more."

"It takes too long."

Isabel pointed out, "Cliff has a plane. Even Tom can fly the plane."

"Ahhh. Tom hasn't mentioned his flying license."

Isabel went on and explained, "He thinks the isolation is wonderful and needful. He lives in San Antonio and relishes the hecticness, but he loves the peace of the ranch. He does understand why you all don't come into town very often."

"I never have."

"How do you stand it out there, all by yourself?"

Chancy shrugged. "It was always that way, and I thought that was the way all of life was."

"Don't you watch TV?"

"Sure. A little." Chancy shrugged. "We work hard."

"I believe your life has been bleak."

Chancy grinned as she shook her head. "It's been fascinating. I've learned so much. The men are tolerant and explain things, when they must, and I'm in a loop."

Isabel chided, "I think you're too tolerant. You're too easy in adjusting to everyone else. You need to direct your own life."

"I do. I have. I'm quite content."

Impatiently, Isabel asked, "How could you possibly be contented in that isolation?"

And Chancy was honest. "Cliff is there."

"How can you be sure he won't leave? Your place is very isolated. Any woman or kids would go crazy in the silence."

Soberly, Chancy explained, "I love the sounds of the winds. I find the sky beautiful and it fills my soul. And we're not that isolated. We get papers and magazines, we have the CB, we have television news, all of which tell of the things going on in the world. And too much of it is awful.

"People are proliferating until the planet is crowded. The people out beyond here are taking the water from the rivers and none is left for Mexico. In the people-jammed Northeast, the U.S. is buying water from Canada. New Mexico and those states are using up the Colorado River and are pushing to pipe in water from the Great Lakes! All that way! Think of it!"

"I'd rather not."

Chancy smiled at her friend. "Too many of the people look the other way. You're not alone in doing it."

Having separated herself by looking away, Isabel looked at Chancy and told her, with some indignation, "I brought you here so that you could see the city of Uvalde. And I find you know more about everything than I do. I came to visit you and bring you up to time, and I find it is you who can tell me. You make me feel—limited."

Chancy was honest. "You're a precious friend. I can't tell you how much it means to me to have a friend who is like a sister. That's the important part of our meeting."

"What if I discarded what worries you?"

"A whole lot of people do exactly that. The earth's population is too large. There aren't enough jobs to go around. Greedy people rake in money and ignore those who need it."

"No good things?"

Chancy immediately replied, "Many good things. People love each other and work for each other and help each other. We'll make it. It just takes time to settle it all."

Isabel replied thoughtfully, "I never had all this to consider. I believe I've been limited in my thinking and knowing what is going on. I can switch the news stations too easily."

Chancy laughed. "Well, I do hope you don't decide to join a doomsday group and chant over all this."

Slowly Isabel smiled. "I *was* thinking of doing

something exactly like that. You've opened my eyes…or maybe it's my brain."

Chancy begged, "Please don't rush up to the Great Lakes and fling out your arms in protection of the Lakes."

Isabel considered and agreed, "Not right away."

That made Chancy grin. She said, "How lucky I am that you came out to visit. I was so excited that you would come here, and terrified that I'd be such a hick that you'd throw up."

"Naw. You smell okay. You even bathe!"

Chancy laughed. She told Isabel, "Having Cliff come to us was a miracle, but having you come to us is a gift."

"Keep that sort of chatter up and I'll embarrass you by bawling right out loud, right here, in front of God and everybody!"

That brought Chancy to a laughing standstill there on the sidewalk. She thought her friend was hilarious.

An older woman came along and said, "I remember when I was your age and my sisters made me laugh thataway. You make me homesick for them."

Chancy immediately said, "Then adopt us into your family and use us as sisters."

Tears came into the old eyes. "I'm uh, uh, Alexandra Petty. I knew, uh, the vice president under—oh, uh, the crippled president."

Chancy immediately remembered things said by the horse-rolled Creep and quickly guessed, "You knew the man from TEXAS who was John Nance Garner?"

Alexandra nodded. "That's the one. We loved him. He was one of us."

Chancy replied, "I'm glad you loved him. He was

fortunate.'' She made no mention of the Garner quotes and the comments on him which she'd read in the collection of the long ago press.

Since Alexandra wasn't entirely sure which way she was going, the two young women walked along with her, guiding her to the friendly lunch counter.

Everyone there knew Alexandra. She'd just forgotten that she knew them.

So eventually, the two visitors had made their purchases, driven leisurely around the town and looked at it. "I'm going to move here." That was Chancy.

Isabel said softly, "Wait a while." Cliff had to have his chance with her. He probably needed time. Isabel wondered how long it would take for him to do more than picnic with Chancy and ride her on his horse. Well, it might not be all that long a time, after all.

Then Isabel said, "If you *swear* you'll watch for traffic lights, I'll let you drive back home."

So being sassy, Chancy tilted her head with heavy thought and squinched her eyes. She said, "I believe I can. I think I can. I shall try!" She lifted her arm and pointed her finger at the sky. She knew drama.

"When did you ever practice doing stuff like that? Nobody in the crew has said anything about you being dramatic. They just say you're quiet and pretty. In that order." She slid a droll look over at Chancy.

"You bring out the inner me like a sister would. I can ham it up, and you don't go hyper or argumentative. How I've needed you all these years. I tried so hard to pass as a male."

Isabel bubbled laughter as she gasped, "A *male?*"

Watching for traffic signs, Chancy replied, "Well, I wanted to be one of the boys. Accepted."

That last word was the one that caught at Isabel. How isolated Chancy had been. "If I had known you sooner, I might not have noticed you."

"I am what I am. I haven't changed."

Isabel demurred, "But you've changed me."

That was interesting. "How?"

"You accept me."

That caused Chancy to figure it out. "You're too good-looking. Women would be hostile."

"You weren't."

"I was just so glad to see a female after all those years. I loved you on sight. You had no choice but to tolerate me."

There was a silence as Chancy drove along watching for traffic signs. She was easy and content.

An agitated Isabel finally said, "I'm not tolerating you. I'm clinging to you."

Chancy discarded that. "You're the leader. I follow."

"That might have once been true. But not now. We share."

Chancy thought about it soberly as she continued, looking for traffic lights. She looked for them in that lacy mesquite area with barbed wire fences, with a two-lane highway through what could be called virgin land.

She said to Isabel, "This 'virgin land' has been tromped through by what all, all these thousands and millions of years, but we call it 'virgin' land because there aren't any towns here."

Isabel responded in agreement, "We're a little strange."

Looking for traffic lights, Chancy mentioned, "I was considering the word...odd."

"That's closer."

"Thank you."

Isabel laughed. She laughed and looked at Chancy. She grinned, still looking for traffic lights. She mentioned, "There are no traffic lights out here."

Isabel sighed with some drama and told her, "There are no crossroads."

"Sometimes in the middle of nowhere, there is a sign that says, 'School Children' in English and in Spanish."

Isabel suggested, "When that happens, there's generally an entrance to some ranch."

Chancy gave Isabel a short glance and mentioned, "You ought to be in some kind of business. You find alternatives. Guess words. Another avenue."

"I'm countering?" Isabel questioned.

"Or expanding."

Isabel considered, then she said with some understanding, "You have an open mind. No one else has such an open mind."

"The men are scared of you because they know you can think. Women shun you because they are competitive."

Isabel blinked. "Now how could you possibly think of that?"

"It isn't difficult to understand. You're obvious. You want people to expand themselves. Look how you figured out how to communicate with Faraday. He was so tongue-tied, and you gave him questions he could agree with or shake his head."

"It was the first time that I ever understood how tongue-tied a man could get. You taught me."

"I'm hardly tongue-tied, being as chatty as I am."

"But you told me about the men being so rough mouthed that they'd shut up and not talk at all. So you were quiet."

"That's basic."

"No. That's...consideration. You gave them the time to talk."

"I didn't have as much to say, and they all knew what all was being done on the place. I wasn't free to interrupt and take up the time they had."

"Don't be so precious."

And Chancy laughed.

They drove into the lane at their place, and Chancy had to comment, "Not but one single traffic light in all these miles since Uvalde."

Isabel stopped her exit of the car, turned with some endurance and replied, "I know." Then she got out of the car.

But Chancy laughed. Her eyes sparkled and danced with lights as she laughed.

And although Isabel turned her head and licked her lips, the laughter rose inside her, and she amused Chancy, who also laughed. They stood on either side of the car, looking at each other over the top and they just laughed.

Cliff and Tom came along. How strange they were there.

It wasn't at all strange. The two men had been watching for the women and getting worried about them. Now the women had returned. The two men could not understand how the women could stand on either side of the car, that way, and just laugh. The two men asked similarly, "What's so damned funny?"

Each woman pointed to the other woman.

There is just nothing more irritating than a woman who won't explain something when an explanation is requested. Unfortunately neither man was committed to either woman verbally, so there wasn't just a whole lot they could do about them.

One male asked, "Did you have car trouble?"

And the other one asked, "What took you so long?"

Isabel was surprised and gestured, "It's still daylight."

While the other gem mentioned, "We went shopping."

Neither reply was what the males wanted. They were a little tense and instead of being worried, now they were a little irritated that they'd been worried. Men are strange.

They were still adjusting to the fact that they'd not needed to worry, the two women were back and okay. They were talking.

Chancy was saying, "We saw a lot of people and the town is charming. I'd never been there. But there were some people I talk with on the CB!"

Cliff asked brusquely, "Who?" Some damned man?

"Lucia, Karen, Beth…even Patty! So many of the people I've known by voice. It was wonderful to see them!" She laughed, very stimulated.

Cliff couldn't take his eyes from her. She was…different. And his stomach was scared. She was trying her wings, and he hadn't gotten to clip them first. She'd fly…how far?

The silent men began to take their women's purchases from the car. The two women were still talking.

Then Chancy stopped and asked, "Is everyone okay?"

"Yeah." Cliff looked at her with curiosity. "Why?"

"How come you all are both up here and not out beyond? It's only 4:30."

Cliff replied, "We…decided, uh, we had to check something out."

Chancy asked, "What?"

More tellingly, Isabel asked, "Who?"

It was Tom who supplied the answer so easily, "You all. We didn't have a time frame for when you'd be back. We got worried."

Chancy replied, "If we'd been delayed, we'd of called."

Cliff scolded, "You didn't take the car phone."

"Oh." Chancy looked at Isabel. "I forgot it completely!"

Isabel added, "I didn't know you had one."

Cliff finally said, "You two scared us spitless."

His sister said, "That was a waste of time. Chancy knows everybody in this whole, entire area." She looked at Chancy. "Was that 'whole, entire' cowboy enough? Am I getting country shine?"

"It's o.k. But you gotta work on it a little bitty bit. Pay attention."

Tom said, "Good Lord Almighty."

Isabel said as she nodded to Chancy, "He's coming along quite nicely."

Chancy considered and nodded minimally. "He'll make it."

Tom laughed, but Cliff was still tied up with worrying about them, and he said, "Settle down."

The two women looked at each other, raised their eyebrows and nodded as they smiled over Cliff's word choice. "He'll make it."

Cliff came to Chancy and growled, "Let me smell your breath." He leaned down, his eyes squinched with temper, and he said, "Breathe."

So she kissed him!

She did that right there in front of God and everybody! Chancy very easily put Cliff into shock. Then she laughed and moved over to get the rest of her things from the car.

Cliff's eye crinkles were white. If he went on thisaway, being so startled by this female, his eye crinkles would be exposed enough to get tanned. Then he wouldn't look so face-naked when he was shocked... by her.

With the two women talking and not even noticing how silent the men were, the four went up to the house with the rest of the stuff. Tom and Cliff exchanged sober, silent communication. What were they getting into with these females?

Eight

Going to the house, the two women were walking ahead and laughing together. It irked Cliff a tad because Chancy hadn't been as stunned by their kiss as he was.

Tom asked quietly so the women didn't hear, "You paralyzed by that there kiss, boy?"

Cliff replied almost silently, "Just about."

Shaking his head in shock, Tom tsked. "That was unduly unkind of her, kissing you thataway in public with us watching every move. She wasn't careful of you. That kind of kiss wobble you too much?"

Searching out the words, Cliff managed to communicate. The wording stumbled, but the words did come out. He said something like, "Be quiet. I'll get, uh, reorganized, uh, pretty soon, now."

That said it all, and Tom laughed in his throat.

Men do that kind of laugh unfairly. Women, hearing that kind of male laugh are ruined. They'll do anything. Another man, like Cliff, just thought Tom's low voice was used in being discreet. Sometimes men aren't too sharp.

Of course, men and women are different. They are pooled together and called human. That's 'way off base. They're really no match. None at all. They never match up right. Not only physically, but in *every*thing about them. From how they walk to how they sneeze. No man would be caught *dead* sneezing like a woman.

Think of walking on heels! No, not the boot type of horse riding, but those heels women wear on nothing-type shoes to dances and to town. Crippling shoes. But the women never limp in public, and they rarely complain. Women are strange.

There was a song once that asked rather pitifully, "Why Can't A Woman Be More Like A Man?" All true. But what would men do without women? Think about that for a while. Assimilating the facts thataway, actually it's facing the truth. It makes a man more tolerant.

The women took their purchases upstairs into the land of magic, and the men were left downstairs, alone.

Cliff didn't mention he'd already been up there in Valhalla. It was magic. He wanted to spend a night with her in that bed. He was intent on it. He probably would have to send Isabel home so he could have a free rein.

His sister was getting too attached to Chancy. Chancy was an appropriate name for the neophyte. He could teach her many things, giving the woman named Chancy, many chances. Most of those would be in learning about men and how they worked. How their bodies worked.

Cliff almost groaned for he was sick with love. Maybe it was just desire. Frustration? How could a grown man get in a situation that was about as difficult as it could be?

To think that *he* was the one who'd urged and threatened and coerced his sister to come out there for a visit! What a dumb thing to have done! Why didn't she just go on back home?

Worse, the two females were good, easy friends! Laughing, shopping, gossiping. When did Chancy have any time for him?

And Cliff's mind was filled with the reality of that kiss, which Chancy had given him, right there, in front of two other people! He'd been so shocked. It hadn't been shock for what she'd done, that part had been fantastic; the shock had been because the other two people were there and watching!

How does a man wish humans to vanish, without having a logical place for them to go, so you can get them back if you really want them back? His impulse had been to make them—just—disappear.

If he had accomplished that, *she* would probably not have ever again fallen into his arms with her soft body against his. Nor would she have moaned, "Alone at last!"

Naw. She would have started calling to the missing two and looking for them, and she wouldn't have paid him any attention at all. In fact, she probably would have been annoyed by his earnest attempts to distract her!

Ahhh. Misery. Misery is how people say the Missouri River. It just shows how things get tangled up.

How had Clifford Robertson gotten into this mess? Well, he'd come out to look at the Bar Q Ranch. The location of which, he *knew,* was too far out away from everybody. But in coming out there just to salve the earnest crew who'd recruited him, he had seen... Chancy. What a name. And damned if he hadn't snapped the bait.

Actually, he hadn't yet *caught* Chancy, who was the bait that sly crew of recruiters provided to slyly have him see. They'd said, "Well, before you say no thataway, you ought to see the place."

And Cliff had gone along for the ride. The underhanded recruiting team had been earnest, supposedly honest men. Actually, they had been earnest and honest about the land and the cattle. But nobody in the bunch had mentioned anything a-tall about the neophyte. That Chancy. That name.

Just seeing Chancy had put a glow over everything at the Bar Q Drop so that just to be there, at the place, it seemed like an award. Everywhere he'd looked, the scene was like a cartoon movie. The recruiting crew had been very tricky, and Cliff had been zapped by a dream woman, and thoroughly trapped.

Cliff thought all that in zips as he'd walked up to the house carrying what-all packages his nemesis had allotted they carry. The other half of the "they" was Tom. He was alert enough to recognize that. Cliff's sister had gotten Tom so mesmerized that he, too, had carried packages.

Men are used.

And now they waited for the two females to come back downstairs. Cliff was in a vacuum. But he slowly realized Tolly was in the kitchen fixing supper. They could hear the gentle sounds as he worked.

Upstairs was where the sounds were straining Cliff's ears. He could not tell what the females said, but they talked and their laughter was soft and very female. If he had any sense at all, he would leave the place.

Could he?

Well, for one thing, his bed was there on that floor just off the living room. If he wanted to live someplace else not so close to her—what other "her" was there?—he could go sleep in the barn with Tom and the horses, the chickens, the dogs and cats and what all else lived out there.

It wasn't a difficult effort to decide he'd stay in the house. Who knew? She just might come down the stairs some night, and come into his section of the house, closing the door softly behind her. Then she would come to him, pull back the covers to reveal his eager, hungry, naked body. Then she'd be all over him. Yes.

Tom interrupted Cliff's mental erotica by saying, "What're we having for supper?"

Cliff's eyes focused on Tom and his brain mentioned what Tom had said, so Cliff replied, "Go ask Tolly."

With Tom gone, Cliff went to the bottom of the stairs and called, "Need any help?"

Both women said, "No, thank you anyway. We'll be right down."

Down on what? Down on him? How like a woman to use a man that way. He wished.

Tom came back with a cloth and a small stack of

plates and flatware, napkins, glasses. He said, "Could you open the door?"

Cliff asked, "What're you doing?"

"Us and the girls are going to eat outside. It won't get too cool for a while."

Immediately, Cliff offered, "I've got some sweaters. Females like to wear men's sweaters." He opened the door for Tom.

Tom replied placidly, "Only in high school, and they have to be the football players' sweaters."

The two were out on the front porch. Cliff pulled the table out from one end of the porch and began to gather chairs as Tom set his burden on one chair.

"Ah," Cliff ah-ed, "so you played football in high school." Cliff began to wipe the table while Tom did the chairs.

Tom was saying, "Naw, I was tennis. I missed the whole shebang, but I survived bodily. The other guys played football, groaned and limped a whole lot."

Thoughtfully, Cliff helped to set the table as he shared, "I remember those days. I even had my own car. It's a vital thing to have at that age."

"I would imagine. I did get to use my mother's car, but it isn't the same."

And Cliff guessed, "Guilt."

"Yeah. Five-feet-deep guilt."

"That's about right. But the depth varies with the occasion."

Tom exclaimed, "You still get guilt?"

"It depends."

Tom sighed, "I wondered about that."

Then Cliff could finally ask, "How'd you convince Tolly to let us eat out here all by ourselves?"

"He'd invited some more of the crew in to eat, and there wasn't room for us, too."

Cliff bit his lower lip. "So us innocents were thrown out to cope with voracious women!"

Tom laughed. "We hope."

The two men put the dogs in the barn. Those were the dogs who walked on all four feet. And they waited for the magic women.

They could hear the light laughter as the budding women came down the stairs, and Tom snared them before they even turned toward the kitchen. He brought them out on the porch. Cliff was on his feet and ready to hold Chancy's chair for her.

Tom seated Isabel.

The women exclaimed at the brilliance of having supper on the porch. "We didn't have a bigger table so the rest of them could be out here?"

Cliff shook his head. "They're out all the time and being inside is a treat. They rejected eating outside." Cliff had such a gentle look of regret.

Chancy started to rise. "I'll go coax them to join us."

While Cliff's mouth only opened in protest, Tom said logically, "The table's too little."

Isabel mentioned, "We could get anot—"

Tom soothed, "Too late. They're eating."

While Isabel's eyes narrowed suspiciously, Chancy said, "We'll plan it better, next time."

It was then obvious that no one should serve those on the porch. The women would object. So the two men went to fetch back the food bowls. The two assumed they'd wait until the men had served them-

selves, and the two sly men would have to take what
was left outside.

Tolly had anticipated the need and filled smaller
bowls and plates with the foods and put them, covered, on a tray. Tom carried the food tray; Cliff
opened doors.

Cliff went back inside and got his boom box and
tapes. They had music to eat by.

None of them noticed there were none of the dogs
to beg and watch and pant. And there were none of
the cats to jump up on laps or onto the table. They
gave Tolly their gratitude. He thought of everything.

How odd to eat on the porch and feel it was a
holiday! They laughed and talked. It was only then
that Isabel really understood how limited Chancy had
been in her self-imposed silence in the midst of the
dinner chatter.

Isabel looked at the younger woman and understood her even more openly. How odd to feel the
pride in her. Well, she was younger than Isabel by
over a year!

The four had a leisurely supper. They talked—a
good deal of which was all of them talking at one
time. They laughed and said, "Hush, I haven't finished!" and they said, "Now wait a minute! Am I
supposed to believe that?" And they said, "Bush-
wah!"

Joe came out and got the plates. Then he brought
their dessert. They were still laughing and arguing
and didn't do more than the automatic thank-you to
Joe, they were so distracted.

The night closed down like a drawn curtain. There
wasn't the northern twilight. It just got dark.

Tolly brought out some ship lanterns and placed

them on the buttresses of the porch. They gave enough light. And the four went on talking. Laughing. Aware of each other.

The music on the boom box was alluring. The men got up and moved the table off behind one of the porch swings. Then they lured the women into dancing.

That wasn't a very good idea. Not with the lamps there. So Tom found another music station and, separated, they wiggled and danced and carried on. They hadn't even had one glass of wine. Their intoxication was in being together and apart from the others.

Out beyond the reach of the lamps' shine, there were "others" who hunkered down beside a mesquite or a hackberry or one of the oaks, and they watched.

Cliff and Tom were aware of the watchers. That was one reason they didn't dance with the women against them. As inflaming as it was to them, it was equally so to the watchers.

A man protects a woman.

The two budding women had no clue they were being watched. They were just exuberant females who did all that moving around—having spent the day in Uvalde—shopping. Ahhhh, youth.

But then, the two men hadn't been idle. And there they were, teasing, dancing solo, showing off.

There is an end to everything, eventually.

As they walked Tom to the barn, the shadows changed. The watchers were vanishing. Cliff saw that.

Tom mentioned that he didn't need a further escort. He would walk Isabel back by himself.

So Cliff said, "Oh, you can do that. Want us to wait on the porch?"

"Never mind."

So Cliff told Chancy, "Tom would rather escort my sister back to the house without us. Do you suppose he has something lascivious in mind?"

And she gasped a little too elaborately and whispered, "Surely not!"

That was when he *knew* he had to have her. But he wasn't as certain that Tom was aboveboard. He could trust Isabel to take care of herself.

But he was going to get Chancy...if he got the chance.

Chancy was saying, "—so I'm not exactly ready to lie down and go to sleep. I'll get a couple of the dogs and go for a walk."

Without even thinking, Cliff said, "No."

"This has been such a day! Going to Uvalde with a woman who is like a sister, and seeing all those people who I've talked to for years on the radio. This is an amazing day, and I hate to let it go. I'm staying up until midnight so that in the years to come, I'll remember it all."

And him...she would remember Clifford Robertson. He would see to it. He said, "I'll stay up with you and keep the...bogey men away."

She laughed, wondering who was going to save her from...him! And she decided she didn't want to be saved.

Following the pair to the barn, they saw that Isabel went inside the barn door with Tom. Uhhh. Hmmm.

So the two stood a way away and talked quietly. Cliff resisted scooping Chancy up and carrying her off into the bushes. He had more élan than that. Surely, he did. Of course. He could be subtle. Naw.

He just wanted to snatch her away and have her all to himself.

She asked, "Maybe we should just stroll along back?"

He smothered a warbling whistle. The barn door opened slowly and just stayed open. Then a tousled Isabel came quietly from the door and walked toward them smoothing her hair. She said, "Lost? Need a guide back to the house?"

And Cliff replied, "Please."

Chancy laughed.

So the three walked back to the house. As they approached the porch, Isabel said over her shoulder, "Good night." And she went on ahead of them quickly. She bounced up the stairs, opened and passed through the door and was...gone.

The pair following her went inside the house. At the bottom of the stairs, Cliff stopped Chancy and said softly, "When she closes the door to her room, come back down."

And Chancy grinned as she said, "Okay."

It wasn't long before Chancy was tapping gently on his opened door.

He immediately opened it wider. His face was serious as his eyes' attention became glued to Chancy. "Did she go to sleep?"

Chancy looked so innocent, standing there with her hands clasped behind her back, her breasts being pushy. She replied, "No, she didn't. She sneaked out to the barn."

And Cliff pulled her into his room as he said in a gasp, "No! How shocking."

Chancy gave him a precious look as she said, "I didn't follow her clear out to the barn."

He gasped, "I'm just glad you didn't witness something lascivious!"

"I'll go back upssss—"

He held her against him like he wanted, and he kissed her hungry mouth like he wanted and held her squashed against his excited front like he wanted. And he dragged her farther into his den.

He was an animal. He smiled. He moved his appreciating hands slowly on her. He sighed. He kissed her just about everywhere. He breathed. His body was going berserk. He groaned some more.

And she led his shivering body to his bed. She explained logically, "I've heard a bed is better for a woman's back than the floor."

And he told her earnestly, "I've heard a woman never realizes that!"

She guessed, "So you don't want your bed messed up?"

"No. No. I was just amazed we made it *to* the bed! You're a wicked, body-hungry woman! I'm terrified! Please, be gentle."

But as he exclaimed all that, he tore off his clothes and then gently, carefully helped her take off hers. He gasped and breathed and his eye crinkles were white again.

"Wait," she said as he laid her down. "I have to assume the position so we don't miss."

He blinked.

"Okay. Now I'm ready." And she squinched her eyes.

Well, now, what man could take advantage of such a brave young woman? So he eased down beside her. His sweat was getting serious. He wiped his face and chest with the sheet, and he kissed her very gently.

He admired her body with his eyes and hands. And he allowed her to explore him while not at all sure he'd survive such a venture.

She was so curious. "I've always wondered how it worked," she told him with great attention. Having been raised the way she was, she hadn't been influenced in rejection. She'd only been told to wait for the right man. For her, it was Cliff. She'd known that he was the right man all along, since he'd come on the ranch.

She was examining his eager member. She asked, "Do you have a name for it?"

"Ambrose."

"Isn't Ambrose rather large?" She lifted the excited tubelike object. "It's rather long."

He knew.

"Why did you name it...Ambrose?"

"We're friends."

She could understand that. But she leaned down and gently kissed it and about blew up the whole shebang.

His reaction and hoarse gasps startled her and she asked, "Are you all right?"

And he gasped, "Let me."

Well, for a woman her age, she didn't have a clue as to what exactly he wanted. So she asked, "Let you? What?"

He struggled to say the whole sentence and be clear for her. He said, "Let me make love to you."

Her eyes got a little serious and she said, "Okay." Then she asked, "What do I do?"

He was sure. "Kiss me first."

And the kiss was so remarkable and she was so

thrilled that he sneaked Ambrose into her gently and she was astounded!

She said, "Wow."

She said, "Well, for goodness' sake!"

She said, "Ummmmmmmmmmmmm."

And she said no other words, but she breathed excitedly and she said some more ummmms.

He just breathed very harshly.

He sounded like he was involved with a terrible chore. He gasped and struggled and strained before he collapsed, with his breathing harsh but slowing gradually.

She said, "My goodness! Well, my word. What a lot of work!"

"Didn't you like it?"

"It was fabulous! How soon can we do it again?"

He pretended to faint.

"I've been so curious. All the animals do it from behind. I wasn't sure how to go about it. You were very good. How is Ambrose?"

"Zonked."

"Oh, surely not. Is he entirely ruined?"

"Not entirely. Be kind."

So feeling safe and very curious, she examined Ambrose and sure enough, it recovered and became very intent. She questioned that. "Why is Ambrose acting that way?"

"You've excited him."

She was astonished. "I was just looking at him. Why'd he get so—pushy?"

That made Cliff laugh helplessly. Ambrose wasn't at all offended. He loved it.

So she had her way. She decided she was in control. She directed Cliff to lie on his back. Then she climbed over him on top and took him, stuffing him inside and riding him down leisurely with swirls and teasing. She rubbed her two breasts on his hairy flat chest and she purred.

She about drove him out of his mind. He had never had such a woman! She was greedy and innovative and a real surprise. She took to sex like a duck to water! She loved it. She laughed softly and purred gently and she bragged on him. She loved all of him and shared herself with him.

She lay beside him and braced herself up on one elbow. The other hand played with the hair on his chest and rubbed his chin and smoothed his hair. He felt he was in some sort of paradise. And he slowly relaxed, ignoring Ambrose, and he went to sleep.

When he wakened at dawn, he began to yawn and stretch, but stopped instantly and his head jerked around, looking for her. She was gone.

Had she been there? It had been so clear. Was it all his imagination? The bed was a mess. It was torn up. Was it all just another hot dream?

Cliff got up thoughtfully and stripped his bed. He put on fresh sheets. He took a shower and dressed. Then he went from his suite of rooms into the hall.

She was sitting on the stairs. She smiled at him as she slowly licked her lips. "I was wondering if you'd get up today. Did I overuse you?"

It was all true. She was his. He slumped. "I'm exhausted." But his eyes glinted in a very naughty manner and his mouth quirked.

And she said with a very fake disappointment, "Shucks. I thought we might ride out to the pecan grove and have lunch together.'' She pretended to rise and leave.

Rather quickly, he said, "We do need to see if the pecan crop will be okay this year."

And she said, "Well, I suppose we could check that out."

In a smothered voice, he questioned, "How'd you get this way so fast?"

She spoke so softly and her eyes were so big and innocent, but she said, "I've been panting after you since you first came on this land."

He sighed very dramatically and chided, "You could have mentioned it to me somewhere along the way and given me some clue."

"I had no way, at all, of luring you off by yourself. You were always busy or gone."

And he told her honestly, "You're so young. You're so perfect. You're why I came on this job, hopelessly, but I couldn't not be around you."

"You've been very subtle," she chided. "I thought you weren't interested. You finally admitted you cared about me when you were so upset because we hadn't called in."

He mentioned, "That sassy kiss about undid me."

"Sassy?" She tasted the word before she admitted, "I couldn't see after I gave you that kiss. It was just fortunate Isabel was there to walk along beside me and get me to the porch. She—"

"My kissing you affected you?"

Her eyes big, she agreed. "You just about blew off my head."

He complained with a frown, "You acted so casual!"

She shrugged in that fascinating way of women. "I was zonked."

He smiled slowly. His face was open and honest. He was delighted she'd been affected...by him! He felt like putting his thumbs under his armpits and swaggering. Being couth, he didn't actually, but his libido swaggered.

He said, "I'll take a blanket along in case you need to rest after we get there."

She put out a hand like a cop. "Don't be so obvious. Taking a blanket? We'll use the horse blankets."

"I *know* you were a virgin, how do you know about horse blankets?"

"I listened when the men talked and thought I was too young to understand."

"What on *earth* did they say?"

"More than they thought I understood. It was not only entertaining, it got me organized so that I knew how to get you."

"I'm surprised you waited so long."

"I didn't love anybody else."

And he asked softly, "So you love me?"

She was surprised. "Why else would I do something that intimate?"

"Curiosity?"

She grinned. "The curiosity has been there a long old time. It was you who made it sparkle. I wanted you."

"Now."

"No. We can't be that rash. We have to be discreet. We'll find a way."

And he asked, "Did Isabel come back inside?"

"She was asleep when I went upstairs."

"Was your door closed?"

"Yes."

Thoughtfully, he mentioned, "I wonder if she opened it."

"No. I put a tiny piece of paper in the closed door. It would have fallen if she'd opened it."

"Would she see it fall?"

"Nobody else ever has."

"How'd you figure that out?"

She explained, "Creep told me to do that when I began to grow up."

"Did anyone try to get into your room?"

"No. They're all good men."

With his voice low and his eyelashes covering his eyes, he asked her, "Do you think I'm a good man?"

She smiled at him and said, "You're perfect." Then she went close to him and put her hands on his chest. She affected him considerably. He breathed harshly. And he leaned down and gently kissed her raised mouth.

From above them on the stairs, Isabel said, "It's about time."

The lovers turned their heads up to see and they grinned at her.

And she had the audacity to mention, "I went in the barn last night, and I think you all have fleas out yonder."

"Heaven to Betsy!" was Cliff's exaggerated exclamation.

And Chancy said, "We don't have fleas on this ranch. You probably brought some with you."

Nine

It was interesting that Isabel didn't go back to her home in San Antonio. She seemed quite content to stay there on the ranch. Her brother was surprised. Of course, Cliff *had* coaxed and coerced and browbeaten his little sister to come out there and help Chancy understand she was a girl.

Isabel had done just that. She had been a miracle for Chancy. A real woman to know and watch and who would listen! One who talked to her. On top of that, they'd gone shopping! In real stores!

And Chancy had learned about traffic lights.

Through it all, the two had become best friends. A man is a little leery of a sister who becomes such good friends with her brother's love. What all did they talk about...about him?

What all would a sister say of a brother? What all did she remember of his early loves? His post-puberty opinions and conduct? His asinine crossover into adulthood?

Early love? Would Isabel mention any of the girls Cliff had thought he'd loved? How did he think he'd ever "loved" any other woman? He hadn't realized what "love" actually *was!* What it is.

He wondered then, had Chancy ever loved or thought she'd loved another man? Who had he been? What boy had lured her eyes and her attention and her curiosity? One of the hands? Her father hadn't been any help or shield to a young girl. She could have done anything at all.

But Cliff had the real proof she'd never made love with another man. And that fact awed Cliff. He had never had a virgin before then. It was a sobering thought. An awesome experience.

Because of Isabel's influence, an expansion of Chancy's limits, now people came to the ranch to see them. That was so strange and stimulating to them all. Especially the crew and the CB-known women who came now.

Only Tolly wasn't rocked by company. He *loved* company. He didn't participate in the conversations, he just baked and stirred and tasted and served and loved the comments on it all.

The women from Uvalde who'd talked to Chancy via the CB came by. It was a delight. And the younger women looked at the men hired there, and they asked them to dances.

Think of that! In a place so isolated that they had felt doomed to be bachelors all their lives or move to another, lesser salaried place. But now they had company! Women came to see them!

The men were exuberant. A couple were taking flying lessons. They liked going to the dances and some places were just a tad far away, by car. Two of the women who visited were from Austin. And everybody knows about the country dancing in Austin.

So until they got their flying licenses, it was Tom or Cliff who flew a bunch here or there for the weekend. And of course, Chancy and Isabel went along.

It was on one of those hops—which was all the time it took by air—that Isabel mentioned, "I've never in my life had so much fun. How was I lucky enough to get to know you, Chancy?"

Chancy replied with amazement, "You're lucky? I'm not sure you're thinking right. I didn't even know how to be a girl until you got here."

And the realization of Chancy's isolation was clear to them all. Without Isabel, she would have spent her life in an invisible barrel of isolation, never dreaming she'd be able to break out of it.

How strange lives go along.

Chancy's hair by then was almost past her ears. She looked more like a girl. She wore a subtle amount of eye makeup, she wore a light lipstick and her clothing was female.

Going around the area or just being around the house, she still wore jeans, but they were those made for women. She still missed all the pockets in the male variety, so when helping on the ranch, she wore shrunken, patched male jeans.

So did Isabel.

Isabel was another woman who had been changed. The change was accomplished by her association with Chancy. It wasn't even planned, for Pete's sake. It just happened. And Isabel came out of her own stilted, unhappy prison she'd made for herself and learned from Chancy on how to share lives.

It had affected the men who saw it all and understood we are all the Captains of our Ships and the Masters of our Souls. It is a serious understanding.

At the ranch, the work went on as it always did. The men worked, and the women visited. The two drove into Uvalde again, and Isabel kept saying, "See any traffic lights?" And Chancy replied, "Not yet. But I'm watching."

They both laughed...every time.

They did their share on the ranch. But Chancy no longer tried to work along with the men.

She found other things to do. She and Isabel checked out the pecan woods. It was too far from the house to be protected. But no one had ever come out there, that long distance, just for pecans.

Once a hand had found there a member of the crew who had been fired. Vincent Moore had come back for the pecans, but the hand had surprised the invader. He'd used his cellular phone and told Tolly who was there. So Vincent had heard the hand identify him. He'd been shocked. Really rattled.

Several of the ranch crew came by plane, with three guard dogs, and were there in ten minutes. The dogs had split like pros and checked out the whole area. Then they came back and watched from various areas, their ears turning at any sound.

The hands had stood observing Vincent's trembling body and shaking hands. They looked at each other, then Rod had told Vincent to take a sack of pecans and never come back for any more.

The crew had then lounged around watching. So

had the dogs. Vincent had been exceedingly nervous. But he'd gathered the pecans from the ground. He hadn't attempted to thrash any of the trees. And having collected a bag full, he'd thanked the silent men, and he'd left. He'd gone over the fence down through another field and over that fence to a truck. It was an old pickup truck.

For some time, the crew took turns watching the area. But Vincent never came back. And nobody else showed up.

Vincent had been fired for good reason. On occasion, they'd wondered what had happened to him. But for quite a while, after Vincent had left the pecan grove, they'd been careful of the cattle, the fences and each other.

They never again saw hide nor hair of Vincent. At times, they'd mused over what might have happened to him and where in hell he was then. He was probably exactly that, in hell.

It had been especially interesting to the crippled Creep that the men were all so loyal to the spread. Not Chancy's father Mel. He was so grieving for his dead Elinor that he had no time to worry about what a flawed, fired hand might do.

People are fascinating.

As with anyplace, the weather was important. On the ranch, they watched whether they got enough rain for the land; that was pretty much the way of the whole country. Whether the beeves got sick or had ticks that were infected, or what all was a constant part of their lives and concerns.

Nobody sweat over anything. They kept the beeves apart in groups, on land allotted just to them. That way, if one group of cattle got sick they couldn't give it to another group. And rustlers continued to bring their trucks to the edge of a place and set out to steal cattle.

The planes helped in that. They got up high and watched. They patrolled. It was a business. Losses and gains. Just like anybody.

It was fascinating to see that Isabel had apparently settled in. The crew wondered and even guessed what she would do when Tom was through with his thesis. They speculated on that. But Chancy moved Tom into the house and Pete took over the care of the horses in the barn.

Tom wasn't sure but that his precious horse shouldn't have one of the other rooms upstairs. It was at the shared supper table that he brought up the subject. He said, "I wouldn't have to worry about him if he was close by."

Isabel said, "Not upstairs."

Cliff said, "Not downstairs."

Jim stretched up his neck and lifted his brows as *he* said, "Not on the lawn."

And Pete said, "I like being by myself so he can't come back to the barn."

So Tom said, "I feel abandoned."

Isabel licked her lips and said, "Not entirely."

Chancy turned and asked Cliff, "Don't you find the people we have around us are a little strange? Only you and I are normal."

And he said, "So you think you're normal."

Chancy gasped indignantly, then chased Cliff all the way to the waterway; and there he picked her up, clothed, and ran into the water with her. She screeched like a banshee. But she settled down and soon she was laughing. Then there was silence.

Tolly told Isabel, "I'd prefer they stayed around. If they did, I could close my eyes. But when he runs her off thataway and she shrieks and then there's silence, I worry."

So one of the hands gave an opinion, as they always did. "Well, go out and holler at them."

Tolly said, "That seems intrusive."

Another commented, "They don't mind. Just tell them that if she's gonna shriek, you wanna know why."

So Tolly did so. And after that Chancy took a cellular phone along and she'd call Tolly and explain why she'd yelled.

Tolly then said to Cliff, "I'm grateful for the word from her, but it makes me wonder if cooking is as satisfying as I thought. I may well go out and court Anabelle Louis."

"I've noticed you eyeing her at church."

Tolly tightened his mouth and lifted his nose as he said, "I'm only courteous."

Chancy suggested, "Bring her out to eat here next Sunday."

Tolly protested, "I'd be in a tither over the food, and I probably wouldn't have time to go to church."

"We'll help."

Tolly lifted his hands and shook his head. "No. Don't say anything threatening like that. I've seen how you cook. Don't upset me."

So the whole, entire bunch at the Bar Q Drop watched the budding courtship by Tolly of the Widow Louis.

That made Cliff chide Chancy. "You gonna marry me and beat out Tolly's being first by getting married to the Widow Louis?"

She gasped in fake shock. "You're competitive."

With that, Cliff asked, "Somebody looking you over?"

She lifted her brows and replied, "Just some roué who goes by the name of Clifford Robertson."

And Cliff exclaimed in shock, "I *know* him. He's a pure man who flinches over naughty words and pushy women."

Slyly, Chancy mentioned, "He might be shocked, but you love pushy women."

Cliff thoughtfully considered that. He finally said, "You're right. But I want sole ownership and soon so I can quit—"

"Sole...ownership!" Chancy gasped.

Cliff protested, "Well, you see, now listen. It's just that I—"

Chancy interrupted, "*Sole* ownership? Sole *ownership!*"

And Cliff said a soft, "Uh-oh."

But Chancy sailed out of the room. And Cliff sat there trying to find a way to think in her way so that he could soothe her down. Why aren't women more like men?

He asked Tom that.

Tom inquired with some interest, "What the hell did you say?"

"Well, it came out that I wanted sole ownership." Cliff stopped and waited, but Tom was waiting for more. So Cliff said, "She got hostile over my wanting sole ownership." There. That was what it was about. He looked at Tom and waited for his response.

"What do you want sole ownership—of?"

"Her."

"Her land? The ranch? Does that include the machinery? The herds? The water rights?"

Cliff frowned and said, "Naw." Then he explained, "I want sole ownership of *her.*

"What did she say to that?"

Cliff said, "She didn't ask. She just got mad and walked out on me."

"Oh."

Cliff waited. "What'll I do?"

Thoughtfully, Tom suggested, "Well, just offhand I'd say nothing, but if she was steamed enough to walk out on you, maybe you ought to pick a nice bouquet of field daisies and give them to her?"

Cliff considered field daisies and then said, "I'll try that."

But Tom said, "Look at the sky. That wasn't in the news this morning."

Cliff squinted his eyes. "Maybe it's just going by."

But Tom said, "It looks serious." And he went off to see where Isabel was to find out if she'd noticed the sky.

So Cliff went in search of Chancy.

However, it rained. The droplets came down and the sky was a variance in colors of gray clouds. It was a miracle. Everybody yelled at everybody else, "Get inside!"

Isabel asked with some concern, "A tornado?"

"Naw."

So she asked logically, "Then why should we get inside?"

And the men told her, "You're a city TEXAN and not a real TEXAN. Any *real* TEXAN knows to get in out of the rain."

"He'll get wet?"

The men sighed. "You can always tell a woman doesn't understand reality. You get inside so's the rain *falls on the ground!* You stand out there and you'll deny the ground the rain. It's raining! Let it rain on the ground!"

"Good gravy." And she went off looking for Tom.

Not the men. They didn't go inside. They danced around and whooped and hollered and carried on like who knows what. But Chancy watched them through a window. And she wondered about Cliff wanting the ranch along with her. He'd rule.

It just so happened, at that very time, that Tom and Isabel rode into the barnyard. The chickens didn't know what to do. They were wet and bedraggled and raising a rumpus over the rain.

The two people got off their horses, stripped off the saddles, opened the gate and let the horses run free in the rain. Then they ran around in the rain shooing the chickens into the barn.

Nobody else came into the barn, so the two went up into the loft. With the rain hammering down on the tin roof, they smiled at each other and kissed.

Tom said, "You're my woman. You understand that okay?"

Isabel lifted her brows and replied, "I'm still thinking about it."

Watching her, he asked with a slight smile, "When're you gonna make up your mind?"

"Oh, when you go back to school this fall. I just might go along."

He questioned, knowing she'd reply right, "And you'll go to class with me?"

Isabel shook her head. "No. I thought I'd go back to my own classes."

Tom frowned. "I'm not sure I'd like that. You want to study or would you like to just be around me?"

She reminded him, "You'll be studying."

"Yeah." He admitted that.

She told Tim, "We'll be together. I'll share the apartment with you."

"What apartment?"

She explained, "There are five kids in my family. My great grandparents bought the apartment house at school a long time ago for their kids. The grandkids used the apartments. Our cousins live there, we do, and our kids'll live there when they go to college."

So Tom mentioned seriously, "We're gonna have kids." Not a question.

"Yep." And she watched him to see if he'd weasel out of knowing her.

He sighed. "I guess we ought to practice."

She laughed as he turned to her. She didn't laugh in a whoop. She laughed low in her throat so that only Tom heard her.

And they made love in the hayloft. It was a perfect place.

The rain continued. The two stayed where they were until suppertime. And in that time, they made love again. They lay back listening to the rain on the metal barn roof.

Tom told his love, "I'll remember that sound and you being with me all the rest of my life."

Isabel snuggled closer. "There'll be other memories that'll crowd that one aside."

Tom frowned. "Oh? What do you intend doing with me?"

"Stick around and find out."

About that time, Cliff went carefully into the silent house. He was a soggy mess. A stiffened Chancy was there with a paper mat. She told him in a stern manner, "Put your things on that paper. Don't step off it until you've gotten rid of those soggy clothes and boots!"

He began to unbutton his shirt. He watched her. She was angry at him for some reason. But she didn't leave. She was giving him time to sort things out and make it all right again.

Cliff asked her very gently, "You gonna be sure I do as I'm told?"

Chancy tilted her head and just said sternly, "That's why I'm here."

"Do you know how much I want *you* and not anything you own?"

She looked at him.

Very seriously, he told her, "I'm not after owning the ranch. It's yours, and I'll work it for you. But it's you I want."

She watched him with equal seriousness, and then she said, "Oh."

After a minute of silence in which she didn't know exactly what to do, Cliff said, "I need a bath."

That put her into something she could handle. She was a little prissy. She told him, "I'm not at all surprised. You were out there hoorawing around in the rainy mud just like a kid.'' She found that she could still laugh.

He said again, "I need a bath."

She considered. She looked aside as she suggested, "You could get the cat to lick you…or—" She looked at his eyes quite vulnerably and said, "I could."

His voice got foggy. "Your tongue's bigger and wider than a little old cat's. It wouldn't take so long."

Her eyelids slid down until her eyes were just slits. And there was the faintest smile on her lips. "Okay."

He got out of his wet clothes in record time and dropped them exactly on the paper mat. His breathing was hoarse and a little loud. And he stood naked. He waited. He was ready. That was obvious.

Chancy's smile stayed slight and pleased. She put out her hand.

Cliff took her hand and led her into his section of the house. He gently closed the door and—locked it. He took her into his bathroom and turned on the shower.

Then he helped her to take off her clothes. She almost hyperventilated, she was so sexually excited.

But then she realized it wasn't her breathing sound that filled the room, it was his. He was so triggered that she realized how intense he was. The whole house could blow away in the storm, and he wouldn't even notice until he'd had her.

It amazed Chancy that he was entirely concentrated on her. And she melted against him as he removed her clothing with no trouble at all. And he had no help from her.

He peeled off her clothing as if she was a precious

fruit that he would consume. Think of the body hunger that gripped him.

She could hear the storm shivering the house. She heard something metal that ripped and then flew in the winds and was hitting along the ground with sounds like cymbals. What was it?

He paid no attention. Apparently his male radar evaluated it and discarded it as not being prime. Only she was prime. He was only aware of her. And he looked at her naked body. He was riveted. Only his eyes moved. Then his hand lifted slowly and gently he slid his big hand down her body, in a swirl over her breast, another gentle swirl on her stomach and then going into the curls of her maiden hair.

She shivered.

"Are you cold?"

She gently gasped the word: "Excited."

And slowly he smiled.

It was some time before Cliff actually realized there was one hell of a storm going on outside. He gently kissed her cheek as he released himself from her pleasure trap, lifted from her and slowly turned over onto his back, just beside her. He put a forearm over his eyes and he said, "You've drained me."

"Good. Then I ought to have some free time for a while."

"Don't count on it, you naked temptress."

"My being naked...tempts you?"

From under his forearm, he nodded a little as he verified his attitude, "—or dressed."

She laughed. "That doesn't leave me any kind of protection."

Quite firm, he told her, "I have protection for you."

"Muscles."

"Condoms."

She rubbed her cheek against his shoulder and lay there, hearing the winds. She said, "Listen to the wind!"

He was silent as he did that. Then he said, "Wow. I'd better see what's going on...outside. You stay right here. Don't move."

But he didn't, either. He was still lying on his back with his forearm over his eyes. And the next thing she heard through the high whine of the storm was his gentle snore.

Think of that! She carefully raised up to see if he was teasing her, in that storm! But he was totally out.

How amazing.

She edged to the side of his bed and slid out a foot and then the other before she touched the floor with both feet. She silently eased out the rest of the way and stood to turn and look down at Cliff.

He was a perfect man.

With great care, she lay a blanket over him, being sure his feet were also covered. Then she pulled on his dressing gown before she left his room and went upstairs to shower.

The storm buffeted even that staunch house. Thoughtfully, she chose heavier clothing. It was getting cold. The house was solid adobe because of the hot summers, but she could feel a chill inside. It was getting very cold.

Chancy had never been in such a serious, long storm. Over the years, she'd witnessed lightning storms, and wind storms and tornadoes. Apparently there were no tornadoes involved with this weather front. It was just a very serious storm. She went around the house being sure all the windows were closed. That was when she saw the snow!

Snow! There was *snow!*

It was being blown and swirled and it was beautiful! How long had it been since she'd seen snow! A snow was amazing in that part of TEXAS! Snow, for crying out loud!

But what about the cattle? What about the thin crews out there? She'd find out if Cliff had sent anyone to help them.

Tolly was in the kitchen as Chancy walked in. Before she could say anything at all, he said, "I know."

With curiosity, Chancy inquired, "What is it that you—know?"

"The snow."

She nodded thoughtfully. "I suppose that's how it'll be for several days and on beyond. Snow. There. I said the word."

But Tolly retorted, "You're number nine. I can see it out the window. I am not surprised. It is there."

So Chancy chided, "It isn't just telling, saying that about the snow is sharing a miracle."

Tolly questioned, "How many times do I have to say that I've seen it?"

"We'll keep count." Then she asked, "Did Cliff send any of the crew out to where the cattle is?"

"I'm the cook. I don't deal in directing the crew."

"Shame on you for being so stilted."

And he was stunned. No one had *ever* challenged him before. Then he interrupted his own thoughts and looked at Chancy. This was the first time she had ever given any opinion or chiding or putting her oar into a conversation. She was growing up!

As Chancy left the room, she underlined that fact. She mentioned, "Get the cat off the table."

The cat? Who let a cat into his portion of the house? He got the broom and, since the table was already set, he swung the broom above the cat and said a loud, "Scat!"

The cat ducked and stayed where it was. It wasn't only on the table, it was licking the butter!

Tolly had a conniption fit; the cat vanished. Tolly closed all the doors to his section of the house and looked everywhere for the cat. It was not there. Tolly's empire was again just his.

Someone opened the door, and the cat was back. Tolly had another fit! The hand was astonished. He gathered up the cat and took it outside and pitched it into the wind and falling snow saying, "Scat!"

So the cat ran for the barn.

Tolly said, "Wash your hands." Then he said to the man, "You may have a cookie." And that dismissed the entire episode in Tolly's opinion.

The hand took two cookies without washing his hands, and poured himself a glass of milk.

Tolly scolded, "You're going to ruin your appetite for supper!"

And the hand said, "Naw." Then he left.

And Tolly looked at the floor and all the footprints of watered snow on his kitchen floor.

Tolly stopped and looked out the window at the gathering snow. And he slowly adjusted to another echelon of tolerance. He might well marry the widow and just leave.

* * *

It wasn't all that long before Cliff came into the kitchen and asked, "Where's Chancy?"

In a stilted manner, Tolly said, "I do not know."

"If she comes through here, tell her I've gone out to be sure the herds are okay and the men have coats and gloves."

"Would you like coffee to take along? I have some large containers."

"That would be just right. Thank you."

"I'll need twenty minutes."

Cliff nodded. "I'll get the coats, gloves and scarves and be right back."

Cliff went out into the swirling snow. He found a hand to help him with a tarpaulin, wood for fires, food and the heavier coats and gloves. Most of the crew had such with them, but nothing to shield them from this storm.

Cliff didn't worry about losing cattle. They were seldom harmed by weather. Of course, with the wind pushing the snow in a curtain, if the cattle drifted off a cliff or into a bog, they'd be lost. But it was the men he worried about. And he grimly gathered the things they would need.

Ten

Chancy asked Tolly, "Where is he?"

Tolly turned and looked at her. She was like a bird ready for flight. She only needed direction. She had just said "he." To her, there was no other he.

And Tolly felt a twinge of jealousy that he was beyond that youthful time. Or was it regret that his own young time had been wasted?

Tolly replied immediately, as if he hadn't had any other thoughts, "He's going out to restock the men, and help."

Without saying anything, Chancy ran to the door, grabbed her coat from her hook and swung it on her. She opened the door to the strong wind and fought it closed again. She was gone.

Tolly went to a window and watched after her. She was fighting her way against the windblown snow as she crossed the yard to the men's quarters.

His horse was there.

As she hurried, she put on her tightly woven, bunched tam under her ten gallon hat, which she fought to keep on her head, as it was then tied down with a scarf. Then she was working on her gloves.

By that time, she was there.

Without knocking, she went into the men's quarters. How like a woman. *They* would screech if a member of the opposite sex just walked in on them, but she just went on inside. Well, there wasn't hardly anybody around. They were out and beyond with the cattle.

With the storm, it hadn't taken the resting men any time to understand they'd be needed, too. And they'd just gone. Who was left?

Hardy would be there. He with the wrenched sprained upper leg. He must be appalled he was locked in there and missing all the excitement. Just watch, he'd try to convince Cliff he could go along and ride in the Jeep.

Working in the kitchen, Tolly mostly watched out the window. He was no better than Hardy. He wanted to help, too.

Tolly got a cake from the freezer. It had been cut into sections before it was frozen. How could they defrost it? They'd eat it as it was.

Putting on his coat and gloves, then tying his hat down with a scarf, Tolly took the covered cake out to the men's quarters. He went to see if he could help control Chancy. She was a handful.

It would have been a routine organization, if it hadn't been for Chancy. As Tolly went inside the men's building, he heard her talking to Cliff. She was insisting, "I need to see if the guys are all right."

And impatiently, Cliff was saying, "It's okay! I'm not rescuing them, I'm just taking out some extra things. They're all right. I have the cellular phone. I'll call you."

"If it's that—routine—then I can go along."

"No. You'd freeze your butt."

And *she* altered it as she said, "No. Mine's encased. Yours is hanging out."

She shocked him. His naked eye crinkles told that. Then the crinkles closed as he began to smile.

There was Hardy's soft snort but he quickly cleared his throat.

Cliff told Chancy, "Keep an eye on Darrell. The ambulance should be here soon. Watch for it. The driver ought to know where to go. But if it's a new driver, he may need directions. Tolly can take care of that."

With his concern for Darrell, Cliff had tied Chancy to the place quite easily. How could she refuse to see to Darrell who was so ill?

Darrell had a chest cold and was right over there in bed. Chancy had heard as he'd tried to cover a couple of smothered laughs and then he coughed his rattling cough. Darrell was why all the other guys were out with the cattle. All but Hardy.

When they'd left just when it was clear there'd be a real and nasty storm, they'd all said that. They'd said they were escaping Darrell's chest cold. They'd be better off out in the wild storm with cold canned food and no shelter than they would be boxed in with Darrell.

Hardy had pleaded, "Take me! Take me along! Don't leave me here with this germ bag."

The crew had dismissed taking him. "You can't ride a horse with that there leg you're limping around on. Since you can't do nothing, you get to take care of Darrell. We'll come back in a month or so when Darrell's well again. So long!" And they'd grinned at Hardy, waggled Darrell's foot at the end of the bed and left with much laughter.

But they'd sobered almost right away. They'd told Cliff. "That cough is all wrong."

Cliff had promised, "I'll get him in to the doctor."

But when Cliff had called in, the doctor's aid had said, "It's going 'round. What are you giving him?"

Cliff told the medicines.

"That sounds about right. He might need a little more help. Can you bring him in for a checkup? I know the weather's bad, but there's a whole lot of people who are ailing. Can you bring him in on Thursday? We could fit him in then."

But with the storm, Cliff had forbidden the women from driving out with Darrell to the doctor. Darrell was sure he'd be okay in another day or so. He was adamant that he wasn't going to any doctor.

Alone, with just the crippled Hardy and the girls, Tolly couldn't handle a determined Darrell. And even as the time had passed, the storm didn't let up.

Cliff had the option of leaving the men out in the storm or getting Darrell to the doctor himself.

But Darrell was then past just seeing a doctor. So before Cliff left, he'd had the doctor's permission to call the hospital.

The hospital ambulance service had asked, "Is he lucid? Can he breathe? Can we wait a day?" With Cliff's replying description of Darrell, they'd said, "We'll get there as soon as we can. We'll call when we're on the way. We've got some wrecks. This weather is bad. Be careful. We've got all we can handle already.''

As he left, Cliff told Chancy, "Don't take him through this weather to the house. He's better off out here. You could kill him getting him out in the cold.''

Hardy said, "I'm here. I can help. I'll watch out for him.''

And Cliff said, "I know you will. But I hate to have you moving around that much with that leg. Take care of yourself. We need you.''

How smart of Cliff to actually say that Hardy was needed. It boosted Hardy's ego and he felt better. He was important.

By the next day, without transport in the storm, Darrell was fading in and out.

The two women had rigged some blankets in a three-sided, boxlike entrance cover so that the cold wind didn't come into the barrackslike men's quarters. Then on strung wire, they rigged a semiboxed, blanket protection around the top of his bed. That way he didn't get any drafts.

He thought it was great. He didn't shiver as much, but he went on fading in and out. It was in the night that the ambulance called in that they were on their way.

Chancy wakened Isabel, and they hurried to dress warmly and went to the men's quarters. Tolly stayed at the house so that he could watch for the ambulance.

The two women closed the door to the quarters and opened the blankets carefully on the side away from Darrell. He was asleep. Or in a coma.

On a chair near him, Hardy slept in a chair. He was okay.

But the women looked back at Darrell.

How did all this go so fast?

It hadn't been all that fast. This was only several days. They'd been too busy to pay closer attention. Darrell was really very ill. And they were alarmed to being spitless.

The ambulance contacted Tolly, who talked them in. Then he had all the outside lights on and listened for them. They did as directed and burped their siren at the gate.

Tolly was dressed like a snowman in the snow. He hunched against the wind and carried a signal lighted lamp, which he swung so that they could differentiate from the regular lights.

They drove to the men's place, then backed the ambulance to the door, got out and went inside. They were very gentle and kind to the semilucid Darrell. They looked sternly at Hardy and talked him into taking off his trousers so they could be sure about his leg.

So the two nubile women went into the box of blankets so Hardy could do as directed without dying of embarrassment. And the interns decided to take him along!

Hardy was shocked. "I'm fine!"

But the ambulance crew was firm. "We don't *need* to come back for you. We'll just take you in with us to be sure. Okay?"

So he went, too.

And the three lonely, concerned people who were left there, watched as the ambulance carried the two men away in the night. They left with the turning red light on the top of the ambulance showing the watch-

ers where they were in the night for some long time.
Then it disappeared.

They closed off the latrines and kept on that heat.
But they opened the windows of the bunkhouse, each
just a slot, to air it out.

They stripped all the beds and aired the mattresses
and pillows. They carried all the bedding to be
washed and put in the first runs in the two machines
in the wash shed.

Then they went inside the big house, stripped in
their bathrooms and bathed themselves, put on clean
pajamas…and went back to bed.

But each one of them thought about the two in the
ambulance. They sent strong support thoughts to them
asking God to watch over them. They lay awake for
a while in the thinking. But they gradually sank into
heavy sleep.

So the next morning, Chancy called Cliff by her
cellular phone. He was on his horse following the
drifting cattle. He asked, "Are you all right?"

"The ambulance came last night and they took
both of them."

Cliff's voice frowned. "Both? Hardy, too?"

"Well, he'd been with Darrell all that time. They
might just want to be sure of him and not have to
drive all that way back to pick him up."

"Surely this storm will be over in a day or so."

Chancy watched the snow blowing. "You'd think
so."

"You all okay? Are you?"

"Yes. How about you? Are you entirely frozen?"

"Naw. The horse keeps me warm in my vitals. My
hands and feet have dropped off."

"If that's all you've lost, we're okay so far."

"What a *sassy* woman you are! You need some strong discipline."

"You could try."

He laughed in his throat in that wicked way men have with women, but then he said, "You'll let me know the instant you have any word about the men?"

"Of course."

"I love you, ladybug."

"Ladybug?"

"You glow."

She laughed softly. Then she looked up and saw Isabel had come to the door and was listening. She raised her eyebrows and whispered, "Tom?"

Isabel smiled as she nodded.

So Chancy asked, "Is Tom around close? Isabel is here."

And Cliff sighed hugely. "Hell, they'll talk an *hour!*" But then she heard as Cliff called, "Hey, Tom? Somehow Isabel has found something to say to you."

And back in the distance from Cliff, Chancy heard Tom say, "Of course."

So Chancy handed the phone to Isabel, grinning at her. Then Chancy went on off to leave their chat to be their own.

Chancy went into the kitchen and said, "Cliff called. They're okay."

Tolly replied, "I called the hospital. They said they'd call after the doctor was there this morning. They're really busy. But they said the men are there. They're taking care of them. They probably say that about everybody."

Thoughtfully, Chancy mused, "This is the first

time we've had a man in the hospital for being sick. We've had them in for falls, rolls, bobwire cuts, shootings, what all. But as far back as I can remember, this is the first time for an illness.''

"Jonny had a blocked bowel."

"Yeah. I remember that. But that was a physical thing. It wasn't a contagious illness."

Thoughtfully, Tolly mentioned, "It's a good thing we have the crew out and away at this time or they might all have gotten it."

"Maybe we ought to build new housing for them. With separate rooms."

"That might be a good idea...so long as they didn't—then—have company overnight."

"Why," she gasped. "None of them would do that."

Tolly just laughed.

After their conversation was finished, Chancy went to her room and found Isabel strolling in the hall, still talking to Tom!

Handheld, cellular phones are a miracle. Think of a man trailing cattle and being allowed to talk to someone miles away.

It was interesting to see people walking down a street and talking on a phone. But the people chatting on phones in cars were dangerous to other cars. The conversation distracted the drivers from their driving. As a result, there were simple wrecks, but there were also very bad wrecks.

How many people walking, talking on phones found themselves on another street entirely? And lost. People do have some trouble doing too many things at once, or being distracted from what they are actually doing in the first place.

However, in the circumstances the men were in, trailing cattle, a conversation at a distance wasn't going to distract their horses from what they were doing.

It was cold.

TEXANS weren't used to that kind of weather. It was rude of New Mexico to send the storm on over into TEXAS and get rid of it thataway.

TEXAS is such a big state for anything to go through. And that included storms. But the natives bragged on the snow.

Who would ever believe that TEXAS would have snow? There it *was!* Right there on the ground in front of them! They made snowmen! And they threw snowballs! Some of the kids even did forts.

The TEXAS people had to go into town to get more film for their cameras, to take more pictures. With the snow, the driving was tricky, which only added to the whole adventure.

Then after all that, in the middle of that very day, the weather changed. It softened. The sky cleared as if it had never been any other way, and the sun came out.

Sun on a spring snow is a disaster in TEXAS. It melts the snow. It drips off houses. It runs down the sides of streets. The ground loosens, and calves are dropped.

That seems such an awkward way to have calves.

Wolves and coyotes jog through the herds looking for a newborn bawling calf that's lost its mama. They're easy pickings.

With the change in the weather, Cliff called the

girls and asked, "You all want to come out and save some of the calves from the damned coyotes?"

All Chancy asked was, "Where are you?"

So she got the ranch map, and he told her the location and what they'd pass and what was around. And he added, "We'll all be watching for you. How about bringing us some of that Christmas candy in the closet?"

It was hard candy that you could put in your mouth and worry it with your tongue for a long time. It was not distracting to a man on a horse, but it soothed him in a trying time.

Most of the men were out with the varying herds. So the two women were lured by each one they passed to come help them.

They laughed and said, "You don't need us. You're doing great!" That was to a man who already had a new calf over his horse's neck and was trying to get the mama cow to pay attention to another new calf.

The cow was insulted, said something in cow language that was obviously distasteful and rude, and she moved away.

With the cellular phone at Chancy's ear, they were directed to the particular group that held Tom and Cliff. The men laughed. "You got here!"

And the girls retorted, "No, we don't want any new, but abandoned calves."

Cliff chided the women, "Only one reject, so far, and Jim's got him." Then he asked seriously, "Have you heard anything about Darrell? Or Hardy?"

Chancy's face changed to being serious. "They're being positive about Darrell. That scares me. And they are—watching—Hardy. What does that mean?"

"I don-know." Cliff's lower lip came out and up over his upper lip. He frowned and didn't hear anything anyone said for a while. Then he whistled and called, "Tom?" And he asked, "Anybody seen Tom? And I need to speak to Peter." He looked around. "Hey, Pete?"

Off some distance, somebody yelled back, "You need Pete? I'll get him for you."

"Thanks! Just yell where he is, and I'll find him."

So pretty soon somebody said, "Pete's out to the right about halfway. A cow's down."

"Off its feet or sideways."

The hand smiled a little as he said, "I think it's a new mama, and she doesn't know what's happening to her, so she's ready to leave this veil of tears."

Cliff grinned, but Chancy said, "Awww."

She rode along with Cliff, leaving Isabel with Tom. She told Cliff. "Are you going to give me calves?"

And he said, "Yep. But they'll be human ones."

"Does it hurt to birth them?"

"I'm not sure. Some creatures have them easily, and some don't. This one they're talking about might not make it. Want to wait back here?"

"Maybe I can help."

So Cliff asked, "You been with birthings before now?"

And she replied, "All along the way. But nobody explained about birthing to me. I thought the cows grew calves by themselves."

Cliff mentioned, "The males help."

"I found that out. Males are really rather useless...otherwise."

Cliff shook his head. "Naw. We guard the grounds and save the women from other men."

"And the babies?"

He nodded. "Yeah. We save them, too." Then he looked over at her. He forced himself to say, "At twenty, you're still very young. I ought to stay away from you and let you ripen a while."

She didn't bother to look at him, she was looking ahead for Pete. But she did reply to his comment. She said, "I'll decide."

Cliff looked at her in some surprise. Just what was she going to decide? And his stomach was scared.

They found Pete, and the cow was stretched out and mooing softly. Chancy got off her horse and let the reins hang. That meant for the horse not to go any distance without her. It stood, interested, looking around and probably making opinions.

Chancy went over to the cow and looked her over rather boldly. Then she asked it, "What the hell's the matter with you? Are you being dramatic? Or are you actually in pain?"

Whatever it was with the cow, she was surprised by Chancy. She opened her eyes and focused on her. She made a louder sound as if with some indignation. She was lying with her hooves lower than her body.

Pushing at her head downhill, Chancy said to the cow, "Get up."

The men said, "We'll help her."

Chancy said to them, "Get away."

Chancy took hold of the cow's horn stub and pushed. She said, "Git *up!*"

And the cow was shocked. She protested. Chancy pushed.

The men came to help, and again she told them, "Git away! If I need you, I'll tell you."

That made the men raise their eyebrows and pull their mouths down as they almost smiled at each other in a sneaky exchange of glances.

Men tend to think they're in control.

But the cow was offended by Chancy's buffeting of her. She put her feet under her and heaved up onto her feet. And the baby calf came out as slick as a whistle! Ah-hah!

The baby was covered with the broken sack. It bawled feebly and it tottered. The cow was astonished. Another cow nearby mooed. So the new mother stretched over and tentatively licked at the mess.

The wobbling calf was plaintive. The mother was amazed. She took another lap at the little mess. Then she looked around as if saying: Look what I did!

And the men clapped and bragged on Chancy. Chancy scoffed, "I've been helping with birthing since I was three. It's no big deal."

Cliff watched Chancy, very impressed. He'd have gotten the cow up on her feet. She was in good condition. But Chancy's way had been better. She hadn't done anything but show the cow she could. That's probably the best thing any creature can know. There are things that seem impossible, but we can do them.

So Cliff told Pete he was leaving and taking Chancy with him.

Pete said, "You can run along, but I think we can use her. I remember what a help she was last year."

Chancy smiled minimally.

But Cliff said, "She's going with me."

Pete told Chancy, "We'll save you all the stubborn ones."

"Don't bother," she replied. "Go ahead and get it over for them."

Pete raised his eyebrows at Cliff and mentioned, "Women are like that. Here's the miracle of *birth*, and they say, 'Get it over with.' No heart." He shook his head sadly.

So Cliff and Chancy mounted their horses and turned back toward the ranch house. They had to take off their coats, it had become such TEXAS weather. The wind was sweet and soft. The New Mexico storm had gone on past—finally.

As they rode along, Cliff said, "Look at the grass. It's bounced up like it's healthy and going to live after all. All it needed was a little rain."

"That was not 'a little rain,' that was a full-fledged snowstorm!"

"Well, it did cool off."

"It froze!"

"You're a picky woman. Are you being thisaway because you got that cow up and birthed in front of all those guys, and you're showing off, now?"

She lifted her nose as she told him, "I've always been thisaway."

"Well, if this is the way you are, I just may have to decide if I can handle a woman like you."

So she said, "Well, make up your mind and let me know."

Then she had the stupid au-das-it-tee to snap the reins and thump her heels on the horse's sides and just…ride on off!

Imagine that!

Well, he was not even *about* to allow a snippy girl who was ten years younger and about sixty pounds lighter do that to him. So he just followed her.

As they ran in that manner, her first and him chasing, he sat back as if it was planned. He did that until the wave of the land put them out of sight from the mob who watched with such interest.

But once over the top of the rise, he leaned forward, batted his heels along the sides of his horse and he said through his teeth, "Let's git her!"

That's exactly what he said, and the horse must have understood clearly, because he straightened out his neck and put back his ears and ran like lightning.

However, when Cliff did that, and the horse's trot changed like that, so did Chancy's horse stretch out. Chancy leaned forward to break the wind's push and they flew along the way...widening the gap between them by slightly pulling ahead.

There is nothing worse than a sassy woman who tries to do everything her way.

Down the way, she ran her horse, and Cliff intently followed. He even gave the horse a slight swat, which offended the horse quite seriously. The horse slowed and looked back at Cliff for an offended minute. Doing that gave Chancy more leeway, for Pete's sake!

So he swatted the horse again and mentioned—through his teeth—that he had other horses to use, and a dumb horse could just languish in the holding pen. The horse stretched out and paid attention. They gained.

Chancy peeked back along her arm and her laugh carried back to Cliff. She was teasing him. He would *have* to get her. And his hungry body agreed.

However, she went into a scattered snow still lying under trees. The horse's hooves threw up clods of the snow, and Cliff had to move aside a little.

She disappeared among the trees, and that straightened him. He sobered and found he was a little scared. He looked for her. For her horse. But he couldn't find her. He came to the end of the trees, and he turned to look back. He couldn't see her anywhere. He was riveted.

He hollered, "Chancy?"

She came from one side, still ahead of him. The horse was breathing and stimulated. Chancy was entirely calm. And she smiled at him.

He sat his horse and looked at her. He said, "You're a handful."

Her eyes twinkled and she bit her lip as she tried not to smile too much.

He said, "I want you now."

And she said, "I suspected you might."

"I have no protection for you."

"Oh, you forgot? How foolish of you. However, I did bring seven condoms."

He gasped almost silently. "Seven?"

"We'll see how well you do."

And he just laughed. His head was back and he just laughed out loud. "You're a wicked woman."

"I thought you just said this very day, that I needed time to grow up."

"Uhhhh." Women find odd things to say at odd times. He said, "Uhhhh," again. He said, "I'll see."

Now that was a nothing reply.

So she said, "What is it you plan...to see?"

"The weather changing thisaway has really gotten to you. You're a real fair-weather friend."

And she stopped as if she'd heard something. She said courteously, "We have to go see Darrell and Hardy to be sure they're all right."

And he said, "Later."

She raised her eyebrows and questioned, "Later? Later than...what?"

"I'm gonna drag you off that horse and do a whole lot of things to your body that will shock you. You'll probably need a day or two to recuperate."

"And you?" she inquired. "How long will it take you...to recuperate?"

Biting his smile with his teeth in his lower lip, he told her, "I might never recover."

She looked around in consideration. Then she told him kindly, "I'll be gentle."

So he swung off his horse right then and let the reins hang. That would keep the horse in calling distance. Then he went to her and reached up and dragged her off her horse.

She said, "You savage." Her delivery was really lousy.

He took his saddle off his horse and put it in a low branch, but he took off the blanket and lay it on the ground.

She was interested. She asked, "You're planning to be on the bottom?"

He replied, "We'll see."

It wasn't quite warm enough when they removed their clothing. But pretty soon they were sweating. He made love to her—perfectly. And she accepted the loving with a hungry body that relished it all.

Hardy was released from the hospital first, and it was he who brought the more fragile Darrell back to the place. Darrell took a while to recover. He was spoiled rotten.

The marriage of Cliff and Chancy was attended by

a shocking number of people. Somebody carelessly mentioned the day, the place and the time on the C.B. The information spread like wildfire.

A whole lot of people considered the leak was an invitation. The entire avalanche of people were a challenge for Tolly. And like any other time, he rose to the occasion.

It was all as it should be.

*   *   *   *   *

National Bestselling Author

MARY LYNN BAXTER

"Ms. Baxter's writing…strikes every chord within the
female spirit."
—Sandra Brown

LONE STAR
Heat

SHE is Juliana Reed, a prominent broadcast journalist whose
television show is about to be syndicated. Until the murder…

HE is Gates O'Brien, a high-ranking member of the
Texas Rangers, determined to forget about his ex-wife. He's
onto something bad….

Juliana and Gates are ex-spouses, unwillingly involved in an
explosive circle of political corruption, blackmail and murder.

In order to survive, they must overcome the pain of the past…and
the very demons that drove them apart.

Available in September 1997 at your favorite retail outlet.

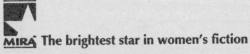

MIRA The brightest star in women's fiction

MMLBLS

Look us up on-line at:http://www.romance.net

Take 4 bestselling love stories FREE

Plus get a FREE surprise gift!

Special Limited-time Offer

Mail to Silhouette Reader Service™

3010 Walden Avenue
P.O. Box 1867
Buffalo, N.Y. 14240-1867

YES! Please send me 4 free Silhouette Desire® novels and my free surprise gift. Then send me 6 brand-new novels every month, which I will receive months before they appear in bookstores. Bill me at the low price of $2.90 each plus 25¢ delivery and applicable sales tax, if any.* That's the complete price and a savings of over 10% off the cover prices—quite a bargain! I understand that accepting the books and gift places me under no obligation ever to buy any books. I can always return a shipment and cancel at any time. Even if I never buy another book from Silhouette, the 4 free books and the surprise gift are mine to keep forever.

225 BPA A3UU

Name	(PLEASE PRINT)	
Address	Apt. No.	
City	State	Zip

This offer is limited to one order per household and not valid to present Silhouette Desire® subscribers. *Terms and prices are subject to change without notice.
Sales tax applicable in N.Y.

UDES-696   ©1990 Harlequin Enterprises Limited

As seen on TV!
Free Gift Offer

With a Free Gift proof-of-purchase from any Silhouette® book,
you can receive a beautiful cubic zirconia pendant.

This gorgeous marquise-shaped stone is a genuine cubic
zirconia—accented by an 18" gold tone necklace.

(Approximate retail value $19.95)

Send for yours today...
compliments of V *Silhouette*®

To receive your free gift, a cubic zirconia pendant, send us one original proof-of-
purchase, photocopies not accepted, from the back of any Silhouette Romance™,
Silhouette Desire®, Silhouette Special Edition®, Silhouette Intimate Moments®
or Silhouette Yours Truly™ title available in February, March and April at your favorite
retail outlet, together with the Free Gift Certificate, plus a check or money order for
$1.65 U.S./$2.15 CAN. (do not send cash) to cover postage and handling, payable
to Silhouette Free Gift Offer. We will send you the specified gift. Allow 6 to 8 weeks for
delivery. Offer good until April 30, 1997 or while quantities last. Offer valid in the
U.S. and Canada only.

Free Gift Certificate

Name: _____

Address: _____

City: _____ State/Province: _____ Zip/Postal Code: _____

Mail this certificate, one proof-of-purchase and a check or money order for postage
and handling to: SILHOUETTE FREE GIFT OFFER 1997. In the U.S.: 3010 Walden
Avenue, P.O. Box 9077, Buffalo NY 14269-9077. In Canada: P.O. Box 613, Fort Erie,
Ontario L2Z 5X3.

FREE GIFT OFFER   084-KFD
ONE PROOF-OF-PURCHASE
To collect your fabulous FREE GIFT, a cubic zirconia pendant, you must include this
original proof-of-purchase for each gift with the properly completed Free Gift Certificate.

084-KFD

In April 1997
Bestselling Author

DALLAS SCHULZE

takes her Family Circle series to new heights with

In April 1997 Dallas Schulze brings readers a
brand-new, longer, out-of-series title featuring the
characters from her popular Family Circle miniseries.

When rancher Keefe Walker found Tessa Wyndham he
knew that she needed a man's protection—she was
pregnant, alone and on the run from a heartless past.
Keefe was also hiding from a dark past...but in one
overwhelming moment he and Tessa forged a family
bond that could never be broken.

Available in April wherever books are sold.